LIBBY'S LIGHTHOUSE

LOVE AT A LIGHTHOUSE
BOOK ONE

SUSAN G MATHIS

WILD HEART
BOOKS

The characters and events in this fictional work are the product of the author's imagination. Any resemblance to actual people, living or dead, is coincidental.

Unless otherwise indicated, all Scripture quotations are taken from the Holy Bible, Kings James Version.

Cover design by Evelyne Labelle at Carpe Librum Book Design. www.carpelibrumbookdesign.com

ISBN-13: 978-1-963212-06-8

PRAISE FOR SUSAN G MATHIS

Libby's Lighthouse is much more than a love story. It's a human story—a heartfelt reminder that the past, whether known, unknown, or even partially forgotten can't define the future nor conquer love. As in all of her books, Susan G. Mathis is masterful at weaving elements of the heart and soul through the intrigue of history and the people of the Thousand Island area. With the vivid imagery from a master storyteller, this first in a three-book series, is complete with the transforming power of forgiveness, hope, and light.

— JAYME H. MANSFIELD, AWARD-WINNING
AUTHOR OF PORTRAIT OF DECEIT, RUSH,
SEASONED, AND CHASING THE BUTTERFLY

Susan G Mathis has brought to life the world of the nineteenth century lighthouse keeper's family with rich historical detail in *Libby's Lighthouse*. I was so drawn into the plights of the heroine, Libby Montonna, and the mysterious amnesiac hero, Owen Shanahan, that it kept me turning the pages. With all their secrets and flaws, these lovable characters are realistic and relatable, as they each discover who they truly are and struggle to move forward from painful pasts. Mathis has gifted her readers another endearing romantic tale of life in the Thousand Islands area. Highly recommended!

— KATHLEEN ROUSER, AUTHOR OF
BOOKVANA AWARD WINNER, *RUMORS AND
PROMISES*

Once again, Susan G Mathis has captured the essence of the Gilded Age from attire to attitudes. Evocative description will immerse you in the sights, sounds, smells, and hard work of being an early twentieth-century lighthouse keeper on the mighty St. Lawrence River. You will be encouraged in your walk of faith as you journey alongside realistic and relatable characters you won't soon forget.

— LINDA SHENTON MATCHETT, BEST-
SELLING AUTHOR *SPIES & SWEETHEARTS*

CHAPTER 1

*L*ibby Montonna sipped her lukewarm tea as she perused the ever-enchanting view from atop the Tibbetts Point Lighthouse. How she loved this early-morning panorama, especially after a late-spring storm the month of May often brought. Minutes earlier, she'd successfully shooed her lightkeeper-father from his perch, pleased he'd quickly scampered down the ladders and the steep steps for a well-earned snooze, leaving her to shut down the lamp at the appropriate time. Until then, she'd peacefully enjoy the stillness of the predawn day.

For her, it was magic!

Libby set down her teacup and spread her arms wide, imagining herself as an elegant white gull soaring freely on the breeze. If only she could fly.

A shame. She pulled her arms in to hug her middle, clicked her tongue, and rolled her eyes. She simply must set aside her childhood fantasies and accept the cold, hard facts of life as they were now that she was twenty. So much change in one short year. So many unknowns. And not for the better.

She returned to sip her tea and chose to savor the slowly

clearing view. The beauty before her brought a much-needed smile and an inner peace she'd longed for since *it* had happened.

Less than two miles across the St. Lawrence River, Wolfe Island, Canada, lay shrouded in the morning mist. To the southwest, Lake Ontario discharged into the mighty river with a constant stream of lakers and salties awaiting their turn to thread through the many Thousand Islands downstream, then make the journey to the Atlantic Ocean—or vice-versa.

Libby surveyed the tower, assessing if everything was in order, if anything needed doing. On foggy, stormy nights like the one just past, her father kept careful watch here in the lamp room, making sure the light burned bright for any vessels that might be in danger. With her sister-in-law and nephew away, and especially now that her mama was gone, Libby was the woman in charge. So, on such nights, she kept the coffee brewing and the prayers coming.

And on these stormy, wakeful watches, Libby would often bake something. Early this morning, it was cinnamon rolls, her family's favorite. Surely, they'd be pleased with the spicy, warm scent filling their cottage with comfort, the still-warm rolls providing a treat.

Though it was still a few minutes early, Libby extinguished the light so she could better watch the magic of the sunrise. With the fast-coming dawn, anyone in peril should spot the shore easily without the burning beacon, so she shut down the lamp and trimmed the wick. Polishing the brass and glass could wait.

She turned to view the river again, and her heart danced at the sight. Puffy clouds raced through the indigo sky, obscuring most of the fading, twinkling stars. The crescent moon peeked out between one cloud bank and another, compelling the rippling waves to glitter like jewels.

Then came her favorite part.

God's paintbrush, dipped in rose and lilac and a touch of pale orange, swept the eastern edge of the water. Muted colors burst through the mist in a kaleidoscope of beauty, pushing back the darkness and dispelling the remains of the evening's storm.

If only He would remove her darkness, her inner storm. She sighed a silent plea.

As the fog dissipated, the pale colors grew more and more vibrant. The stars twinkled their last goodbye. The moon winked farewell. The horizon, illuminated in molten gilt.

And then, voila! Up popped the glorious ball of golden warmth, bathing the landscape with a soft, baby yellow. Glittering its good-morning kiss to the world.

Libby gasped as tears blinded her view. She blinked, then wiped away the moisture with her shirtsleeve before turning her attention to the shoreline.

Wait! She blinked again, focusing on the rugged waterfront.

What was their golden retriever exploring along the rocky beach?

She strained to catch a better view.

What was he barking at? A dead animal? A piece of a boat?

No. It moved! Rose. Stood.

A man!

Libby surveyed the tower to make sure everything was secure. She scurried down the ladders, then the steep metal steps, and then out into the musky morning dampness. She dashed across the dew-laden grass toward the incessant sound of Buoy's barking. The shoreline descended a good ten feet or more below the lawn, and when she got to the edge, the man was nowhere to be seen.

"Where is he, Buoy? Show me, boy."

Her faithful dog whimpered and pawed furiously behind several large rocks, but from her vantage point, she couldn't confirm it was the man she'd seen from the tower. Had it been her imagination?

A groan.

"Sir, I'm coming to help. I'm the lightkeeper's daughter." As she hurried to assist him, the slippery, moss-covered rocks and sharp stones almost tripped her up.

When she reached her dog, a man lay behind a large boulder in the pebble-ridden beach, half in the water and fully drenched by it. "I'm here to help. Please lay still so I can make sure nothing is broken."

The man groaned again and rubbed the heels of his hands over his eyes. When he opened them, icy blues held a glacier of secrets tucked behind them. He quickly squeezed them shut. "Blathers! The light hurts."

The man reached around and touched the back of his head. He winced, his deep, raspy moan tainted with pain. His hand came away covered in blood.

"Be still, sir."

Libby quickly untied her apron and pressed it against his head, both as a pillow and to soak up the blood. She inspected the cut, and both actions incited more moans. "We'll get you all fixed up. You'll be right as rain in no time."

As she gathered her nerve, she took a moment to observe her patient. The widow's peak of his windblown sandy-blond hair flipped into a cowlick at an awkward angle. A day's growth of whiskers peppered his angular jawline and cheeks. Ruggedly handsome, he wore tailored trousers and a fashionable shirt, a fine linen vest, and a pair of expensive leather ankle-cut brogans, now soaked and probably worthless. "What's your name, sir?"

He squinted at her, shielding his eyes with his bloodied hand. "Ach! I'm bleeding." The man tried to rise but immediately fell back. "Blathers! I'm dizzy."

Thick lashes and thicker brows framed his now-closed eyes.

She gently patted down his arms to make sure they weren't harmed. The man's broad shoulders and muscular arms proved he was used to hard work, but they also told her she'd not be able to get him to the cottage alone.

Her brother should be getting ready for work, and Papa should still be awake. They'd have to help.

"Buoy, go fetch Will and Father. Get help."

The dog all but agreed and fairly galloped to the house, barking all the while. Her faithful retriever would knock down the door if he had to.

"Help will be here shortly, sir. I won't leave you. Can you tell me your name, please?" Libby hated how her voice sounded distressed, for she wanted to comfort him. Wanted to be strong.

"O...Oliver? No. O...Oscar? That's not right. My mind's a muddled mess."

Libby smoothed the hair from his face. "It's okay. Stay calm and rest. I'll call you O for now."

"O...Owen. My name's Owen. Yes, that sounds right." He blew out a breath as if remembering took maximum exertion.

At that moment, Will and Father came into view. When they saw the injured man, they scampered down the rocky shore. Will without shoes. Father without his suspenders or spectacles.

"Who is this?" Will scanned the man, the blood, and her. "Never mind. Let's get him into the spare room and out of these wet clothes, or he'll catch his death."

Father pointed to Will. "You take his head. Libby and I will get his feet."

Libby touched the man's arm. "His name is Owen."

Owen moaned and groaned, but he didn't fight them as they awkwardly hoisted him up the hill, across the lawn, and into the vacant, stuffy room. After they laid him on the bed, Father turned to her. "Libby, you need to skedaddle while we undress this young man. Get a change of clothes from Will's room. Might be a tad tight, but they'll have to do. Can't have him be catching pneumonia."

Libby caught her brother's consent and stole one more glance at Owen. Goodness! Even in such a state, he was the handsomest man she'd ever seen.

Buoy sat outside the door, an expectant yearning in his eager doggie eyes.

Libby reached down and rubbed both of his ears. "You're a good boy. You likely saved that man's life. Stay here. I'll be back."

Libby hurried up the stairs to her brother and sister-in-law's room and gathered a flannel shirt, trousers, undergarments, and socks. From the kitchen, she also fetched two towels, the first aid kit, a handful of clean rags, and a pitcher of water. After dumping out the basket of ironing onto the table, she put everything into the basket and scurried back to the room.

Knocking on the door, she whispered, "Please, Lord, let Owen be all right."

"Come in." Her father's deep voice seeped through the door.

Entering, she set the basket on the small table. "How is he?"

Father sighed. "His head needs stitches. Better fetch the doctor. The man has many cuts and bruises too. I suspect it was a shipwreck, but he doesn't remember anything. Saddle up Chief, and hurry, child. Fetch the doctor."

Libby swallowed back a whimper. Father rarely called for the doctor. "Yes, Papa. On my way."

Would the man live? "Please, Lord. Keep him safe."

She simply couldn't bear another death.

Not after the last one.

〜

*O*wen steeled himself against the pain. His head throbbed so intensely that he thought it might be cracked wide open. It hurt to open his eyes. His entire body ached terribly.

Was he dying?

And who were these people? Where was he?

Voices garbled. Nothing made sense.

The two men—doctors? No. They didn't wear white. They stripped him naked, washed him, and dressed him in scratchy homespun clothing, covered him with coarse wool blankets, and wrapped his head in bandages. All the while, he bit back the desire to cry out until a taste of blood revealed he'd made his lip bloody.

What had happened to him? He searched his memory, but disjointed recollections tapped at his brain like an incessant woodpecker outside the window.

Nothing. He couldn't collect his thoughts for anything. The thought of it made his blood surge until his hands and arms tingled. His heart beat faster and faster until he feared it might burst. Then he began to tremble and shake all over. He couldn't breathe.

Even worse, it hurt to think.

The men whispered to each other as they wiped his face and hands with a cold cloth. He couldn't really understand what they were saying, and frankly, he didn't care. It pained him to try to comprehend anything, or move an inch, or take a deep breath, so he lay there like a slab of meat before a butcher.

Was this what dying felt like? Did it even matter? He must relax and let the good Lord do His bidding.

When they began tending to his head again, that was too much.

"Ach! Blathers, man. That hurts." He willed his eyes to open, and before him stood the prettiest woman he'd ever seen,

7

a tall man in a white coat with small round spectacles, and the two men who had undressed and dressed him. He vaguely recalled seeing the woman's face, but from where? Maybe he wasn't dying, after all.

"Does he need laudanum, doctor?" Another woman in a nurse's uniform worked at a table on the other side of the room.

The tall, bespeckled doctor acknowledged her, then turned to search his face. "I'm Dr. Renicks, and this is Nurse Connie. You'll be all right, young man, as soon as I get this nasty gash in your scalp stitched up and stop the bleeding. Drink this. It'll lessen the pain."

Owen surveyed the medicine and frowned. "Isn't laudanum illegal?" How did he recall that?

Dr. Renicks's gray brows rose as he handed him a small cup. "I see you're a clever chap. Well, that's something. The bill is before the Congress now, so I suspect they'll ban it before long. This is all the pain killer I have at the moment, but it's a small dose, so it won't hurt you. Drink up. The sooner you relax, the quicker I can fix you."

Owen took the reddish-brown liquid and swallowed the bitterness. Horrible stuff. Before long, his brain grew fuzzy, and his limbs felt disconnected from his body. Instead of arms, he had grown wings, so he took to flight and soared on the breeze.

Islands, more than he could count, dotted a majestic river. Large ships and sailing vessels of all shapes and sizes chugged upstream and downstream, reminding him of a game he'd played with his friends as a child. The boys had raced each other home from school through people's front yards and backyards. Each one had to weave their way through the neighborhood without crossing paths or they were out. Like those sailing vessels were doing among the islands. He had only played it twice before old Mr. Stallings took him firmly by the ear and reported the trespassing to his father.

And that was the end of that.

Thunder? Lightning? Pain! Was he struck by lightning or by his father? He couldn't tell. But as quick as it had come, the storm subsided, and he kept on flying.

Garbled voices threatened to distract his flight, so he shut them out and turned his attention to the wind whispering through his feathers. He soared into a puffy cloud and out the other side, swooped down to catch bugs on a tiny island, and then dove into the water to catch a fish.

Someone tapped his wing, and he dropped the fish. "Son. Wake up. I'm through here."

He was a boy again. No...a man. He forced his eyes open, blinked several times, and waited for the blurring to pass. Five faces stared down at him.

Dr. Renicks smiled. "Welcome back, Owen. I've got your head stitched up, but you've had quite a time of it. Can you tell me your full name, where you live, and what happened to you, son?"

Owen squeezed his eyes shut. *My name?* He'd already told them, but everything else was fuzzy. With great effort, he opened his eyes again. "I can't remember my surname at the moment. My head hurts too much."

The doctor patted his shoulder. "It's all right, lad. There'll be time for that later. Why don't you rest? Nurse Connie and Libby will stay here and watch over you. You need to sleep, lie still for a few days, and let that thing heal. Frankly, you're lucky to be alive, son."

Owen tried to rise, but a wave of nausea and bulleting pain tossed him back on his pillow.

"Lie still, young man. When you're ready, eat something. But no getting up. For three days." The doctor put three fingers in front of his face to emphasize his prescription. "Three days minimum. More if you need it."

Owen conceded, his head throbbing. "Aye, doctor. Do you have headache powders, please?"

Dr. Renicks listened to his chest before answering. "In an hour, lad. Not right after laudanum. Try to sleep."

"Aye, doctor. Sleep. Thank you." Owen willed himself to relax, but his pounding headache forbade it. The door opened and closed, and then the ladies chattered. If he stayed very still and pretended to be asleep, perhaps he'd learn a wee bit more from them.

One of them clicked her tongue. "Looks like he's asleep." Her voice was deep, friendly. "Let's sit while we can."

Owen peeked at the women, now sitting at the table rolling bandages. Evidently, the nurse had spoken. The lovely lass who he'd seen somewhere before sat across from the nurse and dipped her chin, a gentle smile on her face. Long, shiny hair, black as licorice, framed her features nicely. He closed the slit in his eyes, squeezing them shut.

Where had he met her? He couldn't recall, but he decided to call her Lovely.

The nurse sighed. "Who is he, do you think? From where did he hail?"

"I didn't see any wreckage on the shore when I found him, but with last night's gale, pieces of a boat could have washed far downstream by now. The wind was certainly fierce enough to capsize a small ship. Good thing Buoy was there and I noticed them from the tower." Lovely's voice rang with concern, but she sounded knowledgeable in the ways of sailing and such.

Who was she, and what tower did she speak of? Did he have a buoy with him? Everything seemed so confusing. He had to stop thinking and rest, if only for a while.

The room grew quiet, so he drifted in and out of sleep. For how long, he didn't know. But when he awoke, he was shivering.

He opened his eyes, and Lovely stood over him with a steaming cup of something. "Owen, can you drink a little tea? It'll warm you."

He nodded, only slightly, for even the smallest movement set his head spinning.

Lovely gently cradled his head in her hand and with the other, held the cup to his lips. "Sip slowly, sir. It's hot."

He did as she bid, the warmth a welcome gift. He sipped slowly, not because it was hot but so it gave him a chance to observe her. Her jewel-like eyes, velvety brown, held flecks of gold that sparkled in the candlelight. Two deep dimples embedded in delicate satin skin enhanced a long narrow face with full pink lips.

Lovely, indeed.

"Thank you. Where's the nurse? And you are?"

"Connie had to aid in a birthing, but I've had a fair share of first aid in my day. You'll be safe with me, my brother, and my father. I'm Libby. I found you on the shore. No...Buoy actually found you. I came to help."

"Who is Buoy?"

Her laugh was child-like, sweet and delicate. "Our dog. He found you, and I saw you from the lighthouse tower."

Owen ventured a smile, but even that hurt. "That was providential. Where am I?"

Libby smiled. "Tibbett's Point Lighthouse, near Cape Vincent, New York."

"Never heard of it." Owen frowned. Didn't he know all the landmarks around? He'd studied maps since he was a wee thing. It was one of his hobbies, *that* he remembered. But what was his full name, and where did he come from?

That, for the moment, was a mystery.

CHAPTER 2

*L*ibby readied herself to take the early-morning vigil over the injured man, ensuring she wore her finest day dress and making sure every hair was in place. She even pinched her cheeks a little extra. Not because this handsome stranger invaded her dreams throughout the night, but because she should always look her best when company came to visit. Right? Least, that's what Mama always said.

Grateful her brother had relieved her at midnight to care for the man, by daybreak she was ready to let Will rest. She crept downstairs and carefully opened the spare room door, cringing at the squeak that, thankfully, failed to wake either Owen and Papa. Will must have taken Papa's place in the tower.

She studied her sleeping papa—the man who had filled her life with silly jokes and thought-provoking riddles, dried her tears, and taught her to love nature and life at the lighthouse. He'd shown her how to light the lamp, trim the wick, and extinguish the flame at sunrise. Alongside him, she'd always enjoyed polishing the brass, chattering like a magpie about a lot of nothing while he seemed to hang on her every word.

So many precious memories.

But seeing him now, her poor papa had aged at least a decade in the past year. His hair had thinned and turned white. Deep wrinkles tripled in number on his weather-worn face. A hard edge of sadness and worry now plastered his once-jovial countenance, as if all the spunk and strength and joy she'd always known had steadily leaked out of him. He rarely talked and never smiled.

She knew how he felt, but for a different reason.

That sad day a year ago, her life had been dashed to pieces by an earth-shattering, deathbed confession. Her heart broken into a million pieces. Her family turned into an enigma. Her lifetime desire to stay at the lighthouse and be the first female Tibbetts Lighthouse keeper—destroyed.

All with a heart-wrenching, terrible lie.

Her father stirred and stretched as she stepped into the room. She peeked at the handsome stranger who slept peacefully for the moment. Papa scanned the injured man, too, then rose and quietly left his side, beckoning her to follow with a tilt of his head and wiggle of his still-bushy brows.

She trailed him into the hallway and closed the door. "How is he doing? Did you find out any more about him?"

Papa yawned, then swiped his face with a hand. "Nothing. He's been sleeping soundly and has barely stirred. I've decided that, since the fellow I hired as my temporary assistant keeper won't arrive for several weeks, this Owen fellow can recover here as long as he needs."

Libby glanced toward the closed door, holding back a smile. Wouldn't it be lovely to get to know him by and by?

"I'll help as much as I can. With Alberta and the baby away, the housework is so much lighter."

Papa touched her cheek. "You're a good daughter."

Libby bristled at the moniker as she had for the past twelve months.

"Get some sleep, Papa."

Even that word tasted as sour as a crab apple in her mouth.

Returning to the bedside of the still-sleeping stranger, the weight of the unknown threatened to overwhelm her. Why did everything have to change, especially about how she felt about Papa? She'd always pressed her cheek into his loving hand, but now she cringed. How could she reconcile it all? She had to find out why she'd been lied to and why she had to stay silent and what her future might hold now that everything had changed.

She sucked in a breath as she gazed at her charge. This handsome stranger didn't know who he was either. She frowned, and his name escaped from her lips. "Owen."

He moaned but didn't open his eyes, his brows furrowing in what must be pain. Did he need more medicine?

She stood and quietly crossed the small quarters to the table laid out methodically with all she'd need to care for the man. A pitcher of water and a cloth. A bottle of medicine that Connie stressed he should have every six hours. Tiny packets of headache powders. Rolls of bandages, and more. Her best friend had always been a meticulous girl, and that virtue now made her into a conscientious nurse.

Owen settled back into a restful slumber, but his breathing was shallow and his skin pale. She returned to his side and gently touched his forehead. No fever, but his nose crinkled against her slightest touch.

The poor fellow. What had happened to him? He didn't know his surname or from where he came, and they needed to know.

Maybe she could do something to find out Owen's identity. When Connie came to relieve her, she would wash his clothes and check his pockets for clues. Then she'd go searching for flotsam or jetsam. Perhaps the wreckage of his boat or his belongings would be lingering downriver and tell the tale of who he was and why he'd washed ashore.

Truth was, she reveled in a good mystery, was always ready for a little excitement, and loved exploring the shores of Lake Ontario and the St. Lawrence River. Will teased her mercilessly that she had an uncanny predisposition for drama and danger —though he was just overly cautious. Her papa welcomed her wild curiosity. Her mama scorned it. After all, proper ladies didn't participate in such things. Her mama had told her that over and over, but then, as she discovered, her mama didn't always tell the truth.

Mama...she was a real lady. Born in Waxham, a village in Norfolk, England, she'd come to America at the age of ten. Well-trained in high tea, upper-class ways, and proper etiquette, she all too regularly reminded Libby how she needed to mend her ways and be more ladylike.

Her papa, on the other hand, was a salt-of-the-earth kind of man from Niagara County, and Will followed in his footsteps. So did she, much to the chagrin of her well-bred mama. She'd cried many tears for disappointing her mama, but what did it matter now?

"May...may I have a wee drink of water, please?"

His gravelly whisper made her jump, but she gave him a quick smile and nodded. "Certainly, sir."

Hurrying to the table, she poured a glass of water and returned to his bedside. Carefully lifting his head, she put the glass to his lips. "Slowly, sir. You've been through a lot and mustn't overdo it."

His sun-kissed face accentuated his white teeth and pale-pink lips as he took a sip and licked his lips. She set his head back on the pillow, and when the sunlight peeked through the gingham curtains and fell on his hair, shades of honey butter, cinnamon, and wheat splayed across his pillow.

The sight made her shiver.

His icy-blues sparked a question, despite his obvious pain. "Are you cold, lass? I'm chilled too. Suppose I have a fever?"

He stared at her as she again felt his forehead with the back of her hand. His penetrating gaze sent a lightning bolt through her, straight to her heart. She snatched back her hand, rubbing away the sensation. "No fever. That's a good sign, but the nurse will be here before long to make sure your healing is progressing. Overall, how are you feeling, sir?"

"Call me Owen, please. I feel as though I've been run over by a laker, and my head throbs dreadfully." He smiled, and something flashed across his face, reminding her of warm maple syrup, and those eyes spoke volumes that his words did not. "Thank you, lovely lass. For finding me. For helping me. I'll forever be in your debt."

Lovely lass? She'd never considered herself lovely. Pretty, even. "Stuff and nonsense. It's all part of being a member of the lightkeeper's family."

But was she? That was for later consideration.

She scurried to the end of the bed and scooped up the quilt that hung there, placing it on top of him. Then she checked the bandage bound around his head where a thin red stain had leaked through. As she touched it, a pained grimace marred his comely face, but he bit his lip, yielding to her ministrations.

Owen's brow rose as he closed his eyes. "The light hurts my head, and I'm achy all over. May I have a dose of headache powders, please?"

Libby dipped her chin and mixed the packet of powder into the water. "Of course. Your brogue tells me you might hail from Ireland. Do you remember...anything?"

"I...I don't know. But I've heard that if you're enough lucky to be Irish, you're lucky enough. So, if you say so, lass, that I may be. My head's a jumbled bag of marbles, so I can't be right sure of anything at the moment."

Libby returned to his side, lifted his head, and bid him drink the bitter mix. "It's okay. I hope this helps to unscramble your thoughts. Be patient. You are young and strong, so you should heal presently."

"Aye." Finishing the medicine, he leaned back. "Hope is the cure for all misery. I'd be much obliged if you'd fill my head with stories of your lighthouse. I expect it would take my muddled mind off the pain, leastwise until I drift off to sleep."

Libby smiled. "I'd be glad to, for there's something about a lighthouse that seems to draw people to it. And it's not only that it provides light to help mariners find their way and avoid trouble. It is a beacon of hope, I suspect. I've lived here all my life as a lightkeeper's daughter."

Owen blinked affirmation. "And your mother? Other siblings?"

Libby sucked in a breath. She didn't want to discuss that, so she ignored the first question. "You already met my brother, Will, who is five years older. Another brother, Harry, is seven years older lives in Three Mile Bay, a far piece from here, so we don't see him much."

What if he asked about her mama again? What should she say?

~

Owen nodded, sending his head to throb with a ferocity he couldn't believe. Libby must have noticed, for she touched his shoulder, gentle as a butterfly, and left her hand there. His eyelids felt like heavy weights, so he kept them closed, and his dry throat made swallowing a challenge, but he wet his lips with his tongue. "Aye. And this room? Whose is it, lass? I hate to be takin' another person's bed."

Libby patted his shoulder tenderly. "Oh, don't worry about that. It's our spare room that will be used by the temporary assistant keeper, but he isn't due to come and help until July, so you're welcome to bunk here until you find your feet."

He swallowed hard, holding back a groan, and squeezed his eyes tight. "Aye. I don't mean to be rude, but I can't open my eyes without them hurting. Would you please tell me more about where I am?"

Anything to take his mind off the pain.

Libby cleared her throat, and a tiny chuckle gurgled in her voice. "Tibbetts Point Lighthouse is situated on three acres near the place that Lake Ontario flows into the St. Lawrence River. In 1827, Captain John Tibbetts gave the land to build the first lighthouse that used whale oil and was much smaller than the one we now have. Around twenty years later, the St. Lawrence River locks were built and international trade increased, so the lighthouse became even more important to shipping. Our current brick lighthouse was built several years later and is fifty-nine feet tall. It is tapered from twelve feet at its base to eleven feet at the octagonal lantern room. The parapet and wooden deck surrounding the light are covered with copper, and the walls inside are lined with wood, so the metal stairs aren't as noisy as they are in the unlined towers."

Owen sighed. "Aye, lass. I can picture it all in my mind, and it helps ease my pain. Thank you. I'd be much obliged if you'd tell me more."

Who was this lovely lass, her voice sweet as sugar and melodic as a nightingale? Her words as that of a poet.

"When you're well, you'll have to climb to the top and see the fourth-order Fresnel lens that came from France. It's a beauty to behold. The lantern is huge—a six-feet-wide octagon. It's fifteen feet high with seven lights of thick plate glass as clear as crystal. The eighth side has an iron door to service it."

"She must be a wonder. I don't believe I've ever seen one up close, but I could be wrong."

Would his memory return once the pain subsided? What if it didn't? His heart skipped several beats at the thought, but the lovely lass returned to painting a wonderful picture of their surroundings and filling his mind with better thoughts.

"The light has sixty-one candle power and flashes every ten seconds and then is off for four seconds. It illuminates two-hundred-and-seventy degrees of the watery horizon and keeps ships, schooners, and all sorts of boats safe. And with the lamp so strong, it can get very hot up there, especially in the summer. Do you remember seeing it?"

He licked his lips again. "Nae, I cannot recall. But I have to say that you're the cleverest lass I've ever met, and you paint a poet's picture. The details make me head spin."

Libby sucked in a breath. "Oh, I'm so sorry. I tend to prattle on so. I'll be quiet and let you sleep."

"Nae, Miss Libby. Continue." He could listen to her talk all day, all night. Forever. "How about your family and this house?"

"I'll continue if you'll try and relax. Even try to fall asleep while I'm talking. You simply must rest, sir."

"Call me Owen. Please. I will rest."

"Very well. Let's see. My family has kept the light for nine years. Papa hopes my older brother Will shall become the permanent assistant keeper next year, but for now, he's working on a nearby farm to earn as much as he can for his family. Unfortunately, light keeping pays little, and he wants to buy his own wagon and horse. Will is married to Alberta and has a one-year-old boy, but the two of them are away visiting her family for the month.

"You are in the keeper's cottage. It has this small guest room that will be the assistant keeper's quarters for the summer, and a hallway outside the door that leads to the back porch. Upstairs is Papa's room, Will's family's room, and my room. A large fireplace separates this area from the kitchen, parlor, and office, and it warms the whole house nicely, even in the coldest of winters. And we have a front porch too. Does that help?"

"Aye, lass. Thank you."

Libby brushed his forehead with her fingertips, sending a jolt of warmth through him. "Still no fever. That's good. But now, you must rest. I'll stay here until Nurse Connie comes. Sleep well...Owen."

At the sound of his name, he relaxed, willing himself to rest. Why did this stranger show him such kindness, answering his questions and making him feel safe and at ease? Only a handful of hired nannies ever did that. Not his mother. Certainly not his father.

Wait! How did he know that? Was his memory returning? Perhaps, with rest, he would remember everything.

As he purposed himself to relax, a thick fog shielded him from seeing much beyond arm's length. An overwhelming gale and a torrent of rain accosted him, wetting him clear through. Where was his duck coat? And his boots? The fiery beacon of a lighthouse flashed across the back of his eyelids, and the river quickly faded. The light flashed hope through his foggy chaos, then everything grew still.

The bed creaked underneath his weight, but the heavy woolen blanket swaddled him in warmth. He tucked it tighter around his shoulders, trying to remember what had happened, where he was, where he belonged.

A storm? A house. A woman?

What was that sound? A dog lying next to him yawned, smelling of wet fur and the river.

He tried to rise up on his elbows, but the room spun furiously, so he plopped back down. The creature sat up and nuzzled his nose into Owen's open palm. He stroked the dog's large head and willed his eyes to open.

The dim shadows of twilight revealed a golden-eyed retriever staring at him. Then the lovely lass, Libby, came into view, still sitting by his bedside where she'd been when he last closed his eyes.

"Good evening, Owen. This is your rescuer. You slept the

day away, and that is good. Connie's been here and reports you're stable." Libby studied him with a tilt of her head. She bit her lip and furrowed her brow, then she flung a finger in the air and grinned wide. "Be back shortly. You need nourishment."

Libby and her dog fled the room, leaving silence in their wake.

His head throbbed as he strained to recall where he was, and hopefully more. How did he get here?

That, for the moment, was a mystery.

At least he wasn't smashed asunder on the rocky shore. Thankful for that much, he lifted a prayer for help. To remember. To get well. To know this lass better.

When the door opened, an older man entered.

"Hello, young man. I'm Mr. Montonna, lightkeeper and Libby's father. I suspect you may need to relieve yourself." Without another word, the man slipped a chamber pot from under his cot and assisted him. Grateful for the man's help, instead of from one of the women, he silently thanked God for this kind gentleman.

But as he sat on the edge of the bed, dizziness and pain sliced through him. His head hammered as the bitter taste of bile filled his mouth. "I think I might be sick."

As Mr. Montonna helped him lie down, Libby knocked softly and entered the room. Thankfully, his stomach settled before he made a complete fool of himself.

"I'll leave you to it, then, daughter."

Owen waved a hand. "Thank you, sir. For everything."

The man waved back. Thank goodness he'd covered the chamber pot he carried.

Libby sat down, the tray of food balancing on her lap, eyes sparkling with hope. "I have a little broth and bread. Do you think you can eat?"

Owen ducked his chin. "A bite or two, perhaps, and I need more medicine, if you please."

Libby lifted his head with her left hand and brought a spoonful of broth to his lips with the other. "Sip slowly. Connie forbids me to give you the medicine on an empty stomach."

He swallowed the warm broth and savored the salty goodness. She tore off a small piece of bread and slipped it onto his tongue. It tasted finer than the nicest meal. And Libby's gentle attention made it all the better.

Perhaps he needn't be in such a hurry to heal. Not with this lass as his nurse.

CHAPTER 3

$\mathcal{A}$s the new day's dawn sprinkled sunlight through the open window, Libby breathed in the fresh river air and acknowledged Owen as he opened his eyes. A tap on the door reflected a feminine touch, and Libby grinned. "Come in, Connie."

Her friend entered the room—Connie's uniform perfectly pressed, as always. Her apron starched and white. The nursing cap pinned perfectly to her honey-brown chignon. Though her kind and gentle friend rarely smiled, she was as faithful as the summer was long.

"Good morning, Owen. Libby." She spoke softly, removing her gloves and shawl, placing them on the empty chair. "How is our patient faring?"

Libby viewed Owen, whose lips were pursed shut. "Will said he slept soundly most of the night, and he has no fever. I was just about to fetch him toast and tea, if you both agree."

Connie consented. "A fine idea. I'll check his vital signs and assess him while you're gone."

Libby smiled at each of them before leaving the room. On

her way into the kitchen, she almost bumped into her father. "Good morning, Papa. How was your watch?"

Papa plunked down at the table, tugged off his spectacles, and swiped his face with both hands. His keeper's uniform ornamented with accolades and embroidered in gold made him look rather daunting. "Uneventful, but I'm exhausted. How's Owen? Any news?"

Libby gave him a detailed account while pouring the tea and slicing the sourdough bread she had made the day before. "Would you like tea and toast with strawberries?"

"Yes, please. Do you want me to take a shift with this Owen fellow?"

She slid the bread into the toasting frame and held it over the stove's open flame, flipping it when one side was golden. "Thanks, but Connie is here, and Will can help later when he gets off work. And since I didn't get to scout for clues yesterday, I'm going to search the shores for any sign of wreckage so we can figure out who this man is and what to do about him. I already searched his pockets when I washed his things, but the only thing I can figure is that he is a man of means. Hopefully, I'll find out more while you rest."

Once she withdrew the toasting frame from the stovetop, she opened the cage. Perfectly browned. She slathered a generous portion of fresh butter on each slice and added a dollop of Alberta's huckleberry jam. Then she placed a few fat strawberries on a plate and handed it to her father.

Papa nodded a sleepy thanks, slurped his tea, and took a generous bite of his toast. "Thanks, daughter. I hope you find answers, but be careful out there. That rocky shore can be treacherous and the water still frigid."

"I will." She filled a tray with two cups of tea, a plate of toast with butter and jam, and a bowl of strawberries, enough for both Connie and Owen to enjoy. She'd grab a slice of toast to eat on her search.

When she entered the room, Owen's eyes were closed, and Connie's face was ashen. Libby set the tray on the table, scooting several items out of the way as Connie drew near. "What's wrong?"

The nurse shook her head slowly, whispering so quietly Libby leaned in closer to hear her. "He can't remember anything besides his first name, so this might prove a longer recovery than I had hoped. And his gash is red and swollen. Let's pray he doesn't get an infection. With a head wound, that could be deadly."

Libby grasped her friend's hands and squeezed them. "I *will* pray. Do you want me to fetch the doctor?"

"Not yet, but if he spikes a fever, we'll need Dr. Renicks. For now, he must rest. I'll make sure he eats a little bit when he wakes."

Libby studied Owen, who seemed to be sleeping peacefully. "If you're okay tending him for a while, I'd like to go looking for flotsam and jetsam. There have to be answers. Somewhere."

And if not, then what?

Connie took a sip of tea and inclined her head. "I'm fine here. Take as long as you need. If I need the doctor, your father or brother can fetch him."

Libby gave her a hug, snatched a slice of toast, and quietly exited the room. Seizing an empty bucket, she scurried toward the riverbank crunching the now-cold bread.

Exploring the shore would be tough going, with rocks of all sizes and shapes scattered along the almost two miles of water's edge from Tibbetts to the village of Cape Vincent. But she'd manage. She had to, even with her slippery rubber boots and long skirt. Oh, to be a man and be able to tuck the pants leg into the boots and stay dry.

The grassy clearing led to the rocky embankment and waterfront dotted with boulders, slimy sea grass, and prickly weeds. The crashing waves, chirping crickets, and squawking seagulls created a melodic symphony, and the morning light sparkled magically on the water.

How she loved an adventure, especially one fraught with challenge!

Who was this man? Days ago, when she'd found Owen, he had smelled of river and oil and fish. Surely, he'd been on a ship, yacht, schooner, or steamer. A boat with a motor, she guessed. Perhaps he was a sailor from Ireland? No, his clothes were too grand. A passenger, maybe?

As she made her way along the coastline, she filled her bucket with a plethora of what could be flotsam that was scattered along the shore from midway to the village all the way to the town's edge. But none of it was evidence that the wreckage hailed from a large ship or steamer. The vessel had to be smaller.

Almost two miles of shoreline yielded bits of a broken fishing pole, several pieces of tattered sailcloth, a handful of painted boards likely from a boat, a soggy captain's cap, and several personal items. All flotsam, most likely, for none of those things would lighten a ship's load and be considered jetsam.

By the time she got to the ferry dock in the center of the village, she had filled her bucket, so left it behind a large tree to retrieve later. Libby stopped at the ferry station and told them about Owen. Then she inquired if any of the ferry captains or villagers had found anything of import.

Mr. McDuff clicked his tongue. "Over yonder is a part of a broken mast, I'd say, that washed up on our shore a few days ago after that gully-washer gale. And riggin' got caught in my rudder. I had a dickens of a time untanglin' the stuff. I'd be a guessin' it all belongs to a yacht, maybe thirty-five to forty feet in length. Not a big one, but by the look of the mast's wood, a mighty fine and new one. Keep looking, little lady, up yonder, since the wind had been a blowin' mighty hard in that direction."

The man pointed to the east, so Libby thanked him and continued her search through the village, past the town dock, and up toward the St. Vincent de Paul and Riverside cemeteries. Along the way, she stopped to say hello to several villagers who inquired of her jaunt, and Mrs. Parker told her son to fetch his most recent find—a fine silver pocket watch, now waterlogged and likely unusable. He'd found it the day before, close to the lighthouse on one of his outings with his big brother.

Libby took the timepiece from the boy. "Thank you, Abe. Perhaps it will help our injured sailor remember who he is and from whence he came. If he doesn't want it, I'll return it to you."

Abe grinned, his top two teeth too big for his mouth. "Thank you, miss."

Libby bid them farewell and headed back into town, examining the watch. It was a costly bauble, of that she was certain.

At the corner, Baxter's Jewelers stood with its door open wide. Perhaps he could help? Though she'd never stepped foot in the shop before, when she did, she gasped at the extravagance. Such finery for this tiny village.

Mr. Baxter looked up from working on an elegant necklace. "How may I help you, miss?"

Libby cleared her throat. "Might you be able to tell me about this watch, please? We have an injured sailor at the lighthouse who can't recall who he is, and I thought it might be his."

She handed the watch to the rotund jeweler and waited as he inspected the piece.

Mr. Baxter blew out a deep, onion-scented breath. "Well, now, this is quite a treasure, though it will probably never work again. See here? It was made by the Elgin National Watch Company, and it's one of their most expensive pieces—fourteen-carat yellow gold with this exquisite gold chain. The extravagantly carved hunter casing makes it even more costly. And see here? There's an inscription on the inside."

Libby squinted at the faint etching. "'To MDS. From Father.'"

The jeweler handed the watch back to her and grinned. "If you want to sell it, I might be able to fix it and can take it off your hands for a fair price."

"Thanks, but this may be a clue to a man's past, present, and future."

She waved goodbye and stepped outside just as Mr. O'Neill drove by and slowed. "Need a ride, Miss Libby? I'm heading your way."

Libby dipped her head as she hurried to climb into her elderly neighbor's buggy. "That would be splendid, sir. May we stop and pick up my finds at the edge of the village, please?"

They did, and all the way home, she told Mr. O'Neill about the man, her discoveries, and her hopes for solving the mystery.

But what if this wasn't Owen's watch at all?

What if none of the flotsam was his?

~

Owen awakened to the sleeping beauty sitting on the chair next to him. Libby reminded him of a porcelain angel, her hands folded around something, her head bowed, and sitting prim and proper as if she were awake but praying. She had a spattering of freckles on the bridge of her nose and the hint of two dimples, like the little girl in first grade he had adored so long ago. He'd been so smitten with wee Molly that he wrote her a love note and proposed, even before he'd lost his first tooth. A hopeless romantic, he was.

How could he remember that, but not his surname? Perhaps, before long, it would all return? Aye, he prayed so.

The doctor had warned him to avoid fretting or panicking, for he said it could impede Owen's healing, so he'd followed his orders and tried to not worry.

For now.

The early-evening sounds of chirping crickets, croaking frogs, and buzzing bugs elicited peace in his soul. He glanced back at Libby, and his pulse quickened. She'd been so kind and caring these past few days. What was it about her that drew him from his coma-like existence and caused his heart to take flight like a bumblebee? Even dulled the incessant pain a bit?

He stifled a groan and surveyed the room where he lay. His bed was pushed up against the same wall as the door. To the right of the door, pegs on the wall held a single towel, and next to them, the table and chair where the nurse kept her things. On the wall across from his bed, a plush green chair sat next to a tall dresser that held an oil lamp and a clock from which the rhythmic ticking gave him a measure of calm during the long night. A small, open window with blue curtains blowing in the breeze let in warm rays of sunshine to the right of his head.

He squeezed his eyes shut and attempted to retrieve his past, but the closet of his mind remained locked tight. As if his memories had been stuck in a safe and barred from entry. Or worse, wiped clean.

Where was his family? His home? Did he work? Was he married? Was he a father? Those last two thoughts shook him to the core. He let out a frustrated moan, and Libby stirred.

"Goodness! I'm so sorry. I must have dozed off. Are you all right, Owen?"

Her gaze flashed alarm but quickly calmed. She stretched, rubbed her eyes, and fussed with her hair, brushing back a few stray strands from her face.

"My head doesn't throb as much, but it sure is mighty tender to the touch. Where's the nurse?"

A tiny sigh escaped her lips. "She left hours ago. You've seen

29

sleeping since before she left. But look what I found while you rested."

She opened her hand and placed a gold pocket watch into his. The intricate scrolling on the case revealed it was a valuable timepiece. He opened it. "An Elgin, but it looks waterlogged."

Libby touched his arm, gentle as a breeze. "Sadly, yes. But look at the engraving. Does it remind you of anything?"

He studied the etching. "'To MDS. From Father.' Can't say as I've ever seen this piece, though it's beautiful, like you. Thanks for showing me, lass."

Libby frowned as if she didn't hear the compliment. "I'd hoped it was yours and might unlock your memory." Her voice cracked as she spoke.

"Aye, sorry to disappoint. It may still be, but I cannot recall right now."

She smiled, but it didn't rise to her eyes. "It's okay. I found many other things, but they can wait until you're stronger. Can I get you anything?"

"I could use a bite to eat and a dose of pain powders, please? And perhaps I could get up and sit in that soft chair?"

Libby instantly cheered. "Certainly. I'll be back in a jiffy."

Within moments, her brother Will entered the room. His spectacles and gray hair made him look much older than Libby, the resemblance to their father unmistakable. "Let's get you up and into the chair while Libby is fixing something for you to eat."

Owen slowly lifted himself onto an elbow, trying to fend off a heavy dose of lightheadedness. He shot Libby's brother an apologetic glance.

Will waved it off. "Take your time. I had influenza last winter and was in bed for days. When I tried to get up too fast, I passed out, bumped my noggin', and had a tough go of it. Better to be slow and steady, man."

Owen gradually eased his feet to the floor and steadied himself on the edge of the bed. "I feel as though the wind's been knocked out of my bagpipes, and my pride's sure taking a beating."

Will chuckled, grasping his arm. "Easy does it, Owen."

Dizziness made Owen sway as if intoxicated. One step. Two steps. Five steps, and he plunked down into the deep-seated wingback chair. Had he run a mile? For pity's sake! He blew out a steadying breath. "Much obliged, Will."

"Glad to help. I expect you'll be better in no time. Libby will be here in—"

A knock interrupted Will, and when he opened the door, Libby held a tray of food and a small vase of flowers. "Thought you could use a few pretty blooms to cheer you up. These are the best of my mama's lilacs."

She set the tray on the table, pulled the nightstand over, and acknowledged her brother. "Thanks, Will. I can take it from here."

Will shook his head, tossing Owen a raised brow. "My sister, the hurricane. Have a good evening, and get well. See you later, sister dear."

Libby waved off his tease. "Hurricane. Stuff and nonsense. Have a good night, brother."

The aroma of chicken wafted in the air, and Owen's stomach gurgled loud enough for them to hear. His face flamed, but he shrugged it off. "Thanks for your help, Will."

With that, Will was gone, leaving an uncomfortable silence in his wake. Libby's presence warmed him and unsettled him at the same time. So beautiful. So kind.

He took in a whiff of the fragrant lilacs. "Thank you for these."

Libby nodded, moving the tray to the nightstand in front of him and pulling a chair near to him. "Eat before it gets cold."

Owen bowed his head to give thanks, and surveyed his meal. "Chicken and dumplings. My favorite. Thank you."

"Just leftovers, but you remember it's your favorite? That's wonderful."

Libby beamed and perched on the edge of her chair, prim and proper like a fine, well-bred lady instead of a lightkeeper's daughter. She fairly glowed.

He took a bite of his food and enjoyed the juicy meat, the savory gravy, the soft dumpling. "This is wonderful, Libby. Did you make it? You must be a fine cook."

Libby giggled. "I made this, yes. Will's wife is a much better cook, but she's away right now. I'm glad you enjoy it. What else do you remember?"

For a long moment, he didn't know what to say. Her eyes sparked hope. Promise. But he had no memories to give her. "I'm sorry. I don't even know if this meal is truly my favorite or not. It's a rotten bit of luck, but everything's still fuzzy."

Her gaze turned sad, and she placed her hand on his. The tender touch was warm and compassionate, stirring his senses, and when he looked into her face, he bid his gaze to thank her for her ministrations. "Your hand warms my heart, lass. May I bask in it a few more moments?"

Libby's long lashes fluttered in surprise. Her full pink lips formed a perfect O as she let out a slow breath. But she pressed her hand onto his and held it there a moment longer before pulling it away. "I'm glad I can offer you a bit of comfort in your time of need. It's the Christian thing to do."

A bit of comfort? She was becoming more than that.

More like a lifeline.

CHAPTER 4

*D*ay after day, Libby watched over Owen as he slowly grew stronger. Connie rarely stopped by now, leaving the tending to Libby while Connie dealt with bigger issues in the community.

Birthings. Illnesses. Accidents.

Libby didn't mind.

At all.

She enjoyed many snippets of conversation with Owen, and he often asked her to read long passages of Scripture and poems from a collection she favored. He was the first person in her life, besides Mama, who had ever cared anything about poetry, and it warmed her heart.

Slowly, his dizziness subsided. The wounds healed.

On the fifth day, she guided him to the kitchen for his first breakfast out of his room. But even those few steps sucked the strength from him, and afterward, he took a long, midmorning nap. Yet, much to her delight, he improved quickly with each passing day.

A week after she'd found him, Owen sat in the wingback as

she opened her book of poetry. "May I read you my favorite poem from Emily Dickenson? I love her imagery and turn of phrases."

Owen smiled. "Aye. Please do, for I enjoy her work as well."

How did he know that? It was strange to hear him comment on things as if he remembered when he clearly did not. When would his full memory return?

Would it?

Libby cleared her throat and read,

> *"'Sunrise and Sunset by Emily Dickenson.*
>
> *I'll tell you how the Sun rose –*
> *A Ribbon at a time –*
> *The Steeples swam in Amethyst –*
> *The news, like Squirrels, ran –*
> *The Hills untied their Bonnets –*
> *The Bobolinks – begun –*
> *Then I said softly to myself –*
> *'That must have been the Sun!'*
> *But how he set – I know not –*
> *There seemed a purple stile*
> *Which little Yellow boys and girls*
> *Were climbing all the while –*
> *Till when they reached the other side –*
> *A Dominie in Gray –*
> *Put gently up the evening Bars –*
> *And led the flock away –'"*

Owen sighed, a glimmer rising to his eyes that were no longer icy blue but more a warm aquamarine, though they still held secrets she hoped he'd soon unlock. "Aye. Lovely word pictures. Tell me, please. Is the sunrise or sunset your favorite?"

Libby closed the book and waved her hand back and forth. "I can never decide, I'm sorry to say. From the lighthouse tower, the sunrise is simply enchanting. Its gentle arrival fills my heart with promise and warms my whole day with its memory, especially in the long winter. But on fair-weather evenings, the sunsets over the St. Lawrence are simply spectacular. The drama as it casts its long, shadowy fingers, and such splendor as the blazing, fiery reds and oranges and yellows shimmer on the water. I wonder, sometimes, if He paints it just for me, for it is surely heaven sent! So, to answer you, I love them both."

He guffawed. "Lass, I declare you are a poet in your own right. Aye. I've pondered the choice and cannot draw a firm conclusion either. I believe we are two like-minded adventurers in the same wee dinghy."

Libby sucked in a breath. What a lovely thought!

When he asked to use some shaving supplies, she borrowed her brother's small wall mirror, shaving soap, and straight razor, and returned to the room.

"Would you like Papa or Will to help with the task?"

Owen shook his head, a hint of mischief tugging at his steady gaze. "Nae, but you could."

Was he flirting with her? She took a step back.

He grinned, letting out a deep chuckle. "I'm teasing, and I'm sure you would do fine, but I'd not want to bleed on that pretty blue dress."

Libby laughed. "You're a cheeky lad. I'll leave you to it, then."

He grasped her hand. "Please stay. Your presence gives me comfort. Besides, I need you to hold the mirror for me, if you will."

As a little girl, she had observed her papa shave dozens of times, for she was fascinated by the process. Often, her papa would lovingly declare, "I shave so my kisses will be soft and not scratchy." Then, when his face was nice and smooth, Papa would playfully smother her with kisses until she giggled with glee.

Such sweet memories.

Now, as she held the mirror so Owen could do the job, the thought of watching him shave sent warm tingles down her spine, and she bit her bottom lip, gripping the mirror tightly to steady her quivering hands.

Goodness! Her face burned as she stayed the course.

He nodded his thanks, tilted his head to the side, and started on his left cheek. He kept the blade at an angle and took short, sharp strokes, letting the blade do the work, as her papa always did. His overgrown whiskers came off in nice, neat little lines, and he blew out a steadying breath. He did the same on his right cheek and then opened his mouth wide and curled his lips in.

She held back a grin at the funny face he made, but he concentrated on the task and skillfully slid the sharp instrument over his chin and then down his neck. Like a dance. The allure of it caused her to close her eyes and hold her breath.

"Ahem. Can you please tilt the mirror back up?"

Her neck prickled, and she returned the mirror to its place in front of him. "Gracious, me! I'm such a ninny. Forgive me."

Instead of a scolding headshake as her brother would give, or a *tsk* as her father would deliver, Owen blew a tiny kiss. "It's fine, lass. Thanks for holding the mirror so long. I'm sure it's tiring."

She smiled.

She could hold that mirror for days.

On the tenth day, Dr. Renicks came and removed Owen's stitches. The doctor gave him a clean bill of health, minus the problem of the dark, empty cavern of his memory, which she prayed time would heal. Eventually. The doctor also declared that Owen was free to walk about the property and encouraged him to get regular exercise and fresh air when he could.

Finally.

She'd been itching to show him the light, waiting for the day she could guide him to the tower she loved.

"Shall we take a walk about the property and maybe see the light? It is a marvel. Truly. Few men, and fewer women, are willing to endure the constant hard work of light keeping. Fewer still relish the loneliness and isolation, especially for the ridiculously low wages and long hours. But there's a certain charm to it, a sense of peace and fulfillment knowing one is protecting others on the journey of life. I'm eager to show you its secrets."

Owen grinned. "I've longed for this day. Being cooped up in this small room has challenged my patience. Not that I'm ungrateful for your care and hospitality—from all of you. I am. But I love being outdoors and into the fresh air. Your descriptions of the light have whetted my appetite to see it. Can we go there first, please?"

Libby clapped her hands, thrilled by his request. "With pleasure, sir. This way."

She led him out the back door and down the steps. A few hundred feet away, the lighthouse stood as a watchtower over the mighty St. Lawrence, whitewashed and waiting for them to enter.

She opened the door and waved him through. "Guests first."

Her heart raced as they entered the imposing sentinel.

Would he love it as much as she? Why was it so important that he did?

*O*wen steadied himself as he entered the lighthouse. Not at the great height of it. Not at the metal stairs weaving along the side of the conical tower. Not even at the dark, cool, reverberating interior.

The joy and excitement in Libby's chocolate eyes was almost his undoing.

He'd never met a woman who loved nature and lighthouses and hard work. The women he'd known were concerned with lace and hairdos and frivolities of the feminine nature.

He paused on the third step. By Jove! How did he know that? The flitting, fleeting bits and pieces of knowledge had no cohesion or context. Could he be married? With a family? God help him. How could he be so attracted to this woman and... This is maddening!

Libby reached a dainty hand to his forearm, her brows furrowing. "Is this too much for your first outing? Perhaps another day?"

He blinked. "Not at all. The exercise is invigorating."

Libby blew out a breath. "Carry on, then. But be careful. These steps can be treacherous. And they get even steeper until you have to climb two ladders. Are you sure?"

"Aye. Completely, lass." He pitched her his warmest, most confident smile he could muster before continuing their ascent. "Besides, I simply must see the river from above. I imagine it's like soaring on the wings of the wind, and I'd fancy that immensely."

Libby giggled, her light and breezy response bouncing off the walls like twinkling sunshine sparkling on water. "I often have such dreams. I think they may be glimpses of heaven."

"Aye, I had a similar dream the first day I was here. Perhaps it's this place? I've never had such a vivid dream before."

By now, they had reached the landing to the first ladder.

Libby pointed toward a small window. "Let's pause here, catch our breath, and take in the view."

When they stopped, Owen looked out the window before examining the interior of the tower. What was all that writing? "Poems?" His question reverberated through the tower as if begging for an explanation.

Libby's laugh joined the sound, like a gentle flute to an oboe. "I thought they'd bring comfort and inspiration to the keepers now and in the future. But when the lighthouse inspector saw them a few years ago, he was none too pleased."

"You inscribed them? *I* am pleased, Libby. That was kind, thoughtful, and inspiring. Well done!" Even in the semi-darkness, he enjoyed her warm blush. His comment had hit the intended mark.

Libby shrugged, scanning the walls. "The lighthouse inspector scolded me and threatened to make me whitewash them off. But after reading them, he decided they could stay."

Such a fascinating female she was.

Owen read the quote nearest him. "'The meager lighthouse all in white, haunting the seaboard, as if it were the ghost of an edifice that had once had color and rotundity, dripped melancholy tears after its late buffeting by the waves. — Charles Dickens'."

He paused a moment, memories of studying the author's works bouncing in his brain. But when and what did he study? Where? The details were hidden and refused to be summoned.

For now, he prayed.

"Dickens's works are deep, thoughtful exposés of his times," he said. "His humor, satire, intricate plotting, and keen character development made him a literary genius."

Libby put her hand to her chest, sucking a surprised breath past her pretty pink lips. "I perceive you are a man of astute literary scholarship, sir. How do you know such things? I, too, am a voracious reader, though not so learned. Mama oversaw my learning at home after I turned twelve."

How to answer her inquiry? "There are many ways to learn, lass, and the classroom is not always the best. A wise and learned mother can oft teach more than the most degreed scholar if she inspires and educates a willing and eager pupil. Don't you agree? Shall we ascend?"

Libby consented, waving her arm. "Let's, but take your time."

On the next landing, a small window illuminated another quote that he paused to read aloud. He liked the sound of voices echoing through the lighthouse. Indeed, there was something magical about it.

"'The Lighthouse lifts its massive masonry,

A pillar of fire by night, of cloud by day — Henry Wadsworth Longfellow.'"

Libby placed her slight hand on the painted words, scribed in perfect, feminine penmanship. "A perfect echo from the book of Exodus."

He agreed. "The poet educates with his verse, like so many of his works. 'Hiawatha.' 'Paul Revere's Ride.' 'Evangeline.' They all taught history in an entertaining and memorable fashion. Did you know Longfellow was a professor at Harvard?"

"I do. Yet he was a man of sorrows. His wife died when her dress caught fire, leaving Longfellow to grieve with their seven children until he poured out the last of his grief by writing, 'I Heard the Bells on Christmas Day.'"

"Nae, I didn't know that. I believe we all grieve loss in different ways, don't we?"

Libby swallowed hard, a sad, slight moan escaping her lips. When she spoke, her voice quivered. "Shall we continue?"

He did as she bid, but what deep pain assaulted this fair lass? Her entire countenance silently screamed it. He lifted a prayer for her healing—and his.

As he ascended the final ladder, Libby finally broke the silence with an air of expectancy and joy. "Almost there. Careful now. Your journey is about to be rewarded."

Her melodic voice prodded him up to the top, but how did she navigate the steep ladder in a dress? Though tempted to observe, he diverted his eyes to the spectacular view of the river. "Well, hello, beautiful lady."

Libby popped her head out of the ladder hatch, her voice tainted with alarm. "Excuse me?"

Her eyes sparked...fear? Offense? Anger?

"Pardon, lass. I speak of the St. Lawrence River. Fear not. You are safe with me." He cast her his most gentle, contrite gaze.

She smiled, her shoulders relaxing, her face returning to its soft, peaceful beauty. "Thank you for that. I've never brought a man up here before and didn't want to be suspected as untoward."

"Aye, fair lass. None could imagine that of you. You're simply being a gracious hostess and sharing the love you have for God's great creation. A gift I hold dear. Thank you."

He helped her up to the landing and took in the full three-hundred-and-sixty-degree view, whistling low and long. "I dare say, I've never seen anything more wondrous in all my days."

When his eyes settled on Libby, the sun illuminated her face like an angel. Her hair glistened like black licorice. Her eyes like dark, melted chocolate. His blood surged in his veins, flowed up his neck, and set his whiskers to stand at attention. "Nothing like it at all."

She caught him staring at her and backed up, bumping against the giant lamp. Hard. "Ouch!" She bit her lip and rubbed her backside.

He tossed her a raised-brow apology and diverted their attention. "Tell me about the lamp, please?"

She peeked down at the ladder like a timid rabbit wanting

to scurry from a wolf. How could he be such a bumbling, brash cad? Shame on him! How to redeem the moment?

"I assure you, I shan't ever take advantage or place you in a compromising situation while I have breath in my lungs, so help me, God."

Mirth lit her face as if she might chuckle at his pledge. But as quickly as it came, it went, replaced the most peaceful expression. What a world of experiences he possessed in knowing this woman! A new and beautiful kind of world, he suspected.

Libby's sweet voice broke into his thoughts. "If you think this delectable, you'll have to return to see the sunrise and sunset. Oh, look there? A saltie!"

She pointed to a sea-going ship with mounds of logs covering its deck. A dozen smaller vessels gave way to the large one. Sailors bustled about as it threaded through the passage between this shoreline and the island beyond.

"That land mass over yonder is Wolfe Island, Canada. It's the biggest island in the Thousand Islands. You can take a ferry from the village to the island and be in another country within the hour. Isn't that grand?"

"Aye, I think I've been to Canada before, though I don't recall any details. This present condition is infuriating." His voice sounded flat, exasperated, even to his own ears. But enough of him. "Continue?"

Libby touched the huge lamp. "This Fresnel lens uses glass prisms to change the direction of multiple beams of light, so they all come together into one strong beam that warns sailors of danger, saves lives, and creates something beautiful. Perhaps you are on such a journey, Owen. All those scattered memories and thoughts will soon come together."

A sheen of tears glistened in her eyes. "Perhaps the light will soon shine on your memories and dispel your darkness."

"Thank you for that. I confess, I am rather discouraged

about it. But enough sadness. The fine details you share makes my head spin."

Her pretty face slipped into dismay. "I'm sorry. I didn't mean to bring unease."

"You misunderstand, fair lass. You are such an enigma of feminine beauty mixed with the brilliance of a university scholar. And add to that your love of this place, nature, and the river. That is the tantalizing brew that makes me dizzy."

That, and her beauty, inside and out.

CHAPTER 5

*G*oodness! Libby's heart beat so strong she feared the sound might echo off the lamp room windows like a gong. She sucked in several deep breaths to calm it, but that didn't help. Not one bit.

A waft of sandalwood set her nerves to tingle. Her papa's cologne, but it smelled rather different on Owen. Quite nice, actually. Warm and inviting.

She'd never encountered such a learned man who enjoyed poetry and liked the same authors she did. Besides, the way he spoke only confirmed that he had to be an educated, upper-class gentleman. And affirming her love of learning? She wanted to hug him for that.

Her papa scoffed at Mama's insistence on giving her an education beyond the one-room schoolhouse she had attended. Her brother Will teased her mercilessly, especially about the poems she loved and wrote on the walls.

"Libby? Is that you up there? Is someone with you?"

What was Will doing home at this hour? He should still be working at the Grayson farm. She'd never hear the end of her bringing a man up here.

"Yes, it's me. I'm showing Owen the light and the views from up here." Despite her best efforts, her voice quivered, her cheeks burning.

"I'll be right up." Will's words and footfalls revealed he was already ascending the tower. Fast.

Owen appeared unconcerned with Will joining them, for he pointed out the window. "What's that white pennant flying on the flagpole down there? It's bordered with red and bearing a black lighthouse. Some distress signal or warning?"

She assumed her most professional posture. "It is a badge of honor. My papa received the Service as an Efficiency pennant for being the best-kept and neatest light and grounds of the seventy-five lighthouses between Detroit and Ogdensburg. Can you imagine? It is quite prestigious."

At that moment, her brother poked his head in through the opening and climbed the ladder to join them in the narrow deck of the lantern room. "And when Papa retires, I'll be taking over the keeper duties. I plan to earn one too."

Will, just five years older than herself, had already gone prematurely gray, but he maintained a well-trimmed beard and had a handsome face. He wore spectacles that reminded her of their father, though he was still, and would always be, her teasing, uptight, and overly cautious brother.

"Jolly good, sir. I hope you do." Owen put out his hand.

Her brother shook it, cast her a mischievous grin, and crooked a thumb at her. "Has she been talking your ear off? She prattles on when she gets all high and mighty up here in the tower."

Owen cast her a kind smile. "On the contrary. Your sister has a keen and witty mind. One, I must admit, like I've never before encountered. Even in my days at university."

Will's eyebrows furrowed. "You've attended university? Where?"

Owen rubbed his temples. "I don't understand how my

45

mind is working—and not working—since the accident. A tiny memory flits in and then retreats, like an incessant lightning bug in the dead of night. And then a thought slips off my tongue, and I cannot logically verify it. I reckon it to be true, or I would not have thought it, aye?"

Libby interrupted them. "Please don't fret about it, Owen. You're still healing, and I trust everything will be sorted out in due time."

Owen touched her arm and gently patted it. "Thank you for that. I shall endeavor to be patient."

Her brother's eyes narrowed as he stared at Owen's hand on her arm, his lips pursing with objection at the intimate touch. He shook his head at her, ignoring Owen. "You'd best be getting down before you tucker him out. That ladder and steep descent is no place for a recuperating sick man. Really, Libby. You should know better."

She opened her mouth to reply, but Owen squared his shoulders and stood even straighter than he already was, as if encountering an adversary. "Nae, she discouraged this jaunt, Will." He waved his arm toward the window. "But after her wonderful descriptions of this view—which were entirely accurate and wonderful, I might add—it is I who practically demanded to see it and the light. I'll be fine, I can assure you. But if it is your pleasure, I will go now, and I thank both of you for allowing me to intrude on this magical space."

Will concurred. "I have a few things to do here for Papa. Good day to you."

Miffed by her brother's cold retort, Libby tossed him a grimace and followed Owen down the ladder. "See you later, Will. And I hope you'll be in a better mood."

Her brother turned his back to her and didn't respond.

Halfway down the steep set of steps, Owen stopped to read another poem on the wall.

"'A far-off light across the waste, As dim as dim might be,

That came and went like a lighthouse gleam

On a black night at sea. — William Cosmo Monkhouse, British poet.' I'm not familiar with this poem or the poet."

Libby smiled. "I read he's become an acclaimed art critic in Britain. He's the poet who wrote, 'The Christ upon the Hill.' Do you know it?"

Owen whistled, adding a quick shake of his head. "Do you? Aye, I dare say I've met no one like you, Libby."

She shrugged. "My mama was British and loved literature. She taught me well."

"Indeed, she did. Every lassie should have such a mother."

Suddenly, her breakfast soured in her stomach, and a shiver slipped up her spine and set the fine hairs on the nape of her neck to prickle. Her mama should have taught her daughter who she really was and from whence she came instead of hiding secrets all these years. That would have been the education she needed most.

Claustrophobia threatened to cut off her air supply, so she slipped past Owen and hurried down the circular metal stairs that led to the base of the tower as fast as she could. The vibrating iron stairs sent shivers through her feet and up to her heart. The stench of kerosene, pungent and oily, accosted her nose and threatened to give her a headache. Though Owen's footsteps rang behind her, she didn't turn to check on him. She needed fresh air to dispel the sudden gloom of hurtful memories and to keep the threatening tears at bay. How quickly things could change when memories of Mama arose!

She rushed outside and gulped in a breath. She closed her eyes and tried to will the hurt away and squeeze back the tears before Owen noticed.

"Did I offend you, lass? If so, I am truly sorry. Perhaps it is time for me to leave and let all of you find peace. I fear I've somehow upset you, exasperated your brother, and put an undue burden on your papa. Surely, I can find a room in the village until I discover where I belong."

Libby gazed up at the dejected man, her throat constricting as if being choked. Where he belonged? Where did *she* belong? They were both in an all-too-similar quandary.

She shook her head. "Keeping the lighthouse and being a part of the keeper's family isn't only about lighting the lamp. At times, it's helping others through a difficult season of life. Praying for their recovery. Trusting they'll be all right. That is not only our duty but also our God-given honor."

"Aye, and I thank you for that. But I've imposed upon you for far too long."

Libby placed her hand on his forearm. "Please stay. You have yet to know where your family is, and, I'm sorry to say, you have no money for a room. Papa said you have a welcome place here. Besides, you still have healing to do."

Will stepped into the sunshine. She hadn't even heard him coming. "May I have a word, sister?" His words reeked of anger.

She removed her hand from Owen's arm and followed her brother toward the river's edge. What was wrong with him? What happened to the work he had to do for Papa?

When she and Will got to the embankment, she turned to see Owen climb the steps to the keeper's house and go inside.

Will grabbed her arm and shook it. "What do you think you're doing, Elizabeth Montonna?"

"What? What am I doing that irks you so? I didn't realize I couldn't bring a friend up into the tower to see the views of the river. Papa certainly wouldn't mind."

Her brother gave her arm another shake before letting go. He groaned loudly, rolling his eyes in disdain. "Friend? Is that what you call him? I thought he was a patient, a stranger who lost his memory. Lord only knows who he might really be. A pirate? A swindler? A rogue?"

Libby guffawed sarcastically. "Oh please. If you haven't realized Owen is a kind and grateful gentleman who needs our help, then you are terribly misguided."

Will put his hand firmly around her shoulder and cuddled up to her, pretending to flirt with her. "And what was all that touching and batting your eyelashes I saw? And him touching you! The rogue needs a good horsewhipping."

For several moments, Libby struggled to find her composure and not lash out at her brother as he had with her.

Do unto others as you'd have them do unto you.

She willed her voice steady as she pulled away from him. "Owen has never been inappropriate with me, and I have not flirted with him. He has only ever been respectful and grateful for our help. I am offended at the very suggestion of it, Will. You should mind your own business. You are not my papa!"

With that, she turned on her heel and hurried away to walk off her angst along the soothing shore of the St. Lawrence River.

But *was* Owen flirting with her?

Was she with him?

~

*O*wen dreamed of the dark-haired lass all night. Libby had swept in, capturing his heart and mind—what there was of it—in two shakes of a lamb's tail.

The next morning, she joined him on the porch wearing a radiating grin and a broad-brimmed, floppy straw hat with a wide yellow ribbon, and she was prettier than ever. Ivory skin. Full pink lips. Darling dimples. Eyes as warm as a midsummer's day.

Her willowy, womanly figure made it challenging to avert his eyes. And best of all, she hadn't a clue she was so breathtakingly lovely.

"Good day to you, Owen. Did you rest well?" Her tone lit up

the morning as if it had been painted as yellow as the ribbons she wore.

"Aye, and top of the morning to you, fair lass." He stood and waved a hand toward the lighthouse grounds. "Join me on a walk? I'm feeling stronger every day, and the more I exercise, the better I feel. If only my memory would return, I'd be fit as a fiddle."

The compassion in Libby's eyes eased his anxiety in a moment. "It's a perfect time for a quick stroll before breakfast. I love watching nature awaken to a new day. Birds singing their morning songs. Bees buzzing in the flowering bushes. The morning sun dancing on the river. The promise of fresh mercies. It's magical."

"I agree. I cannot recall why, but I believe I also enjoy being on the water in the morning. It's one of those flitting feelings I keep getting, and I must say, it's rather vexing."

Libby sighed as they walked toward the barn. "I'm so sorry you're struggling with this, but Dr. Renicks urges patience. He also said you'll likely recover your memories in time, but it's an untested science, so he doesn't know when or how. I pray that God will return it all to you very soon. After all, He's the Great Physician."

"Thanks for reminding me of that. I'll be patient and trust God." He stopped and put a hand to his ear. "Listen to that pileated woodpecker. The series of notes in its long, loud call sound as though someone is laughing at us."

They chuckled together, and he honed in on more bird calls in the distance. "What do you hear?"

"I hear a cardinal and a robin. Papa taught me many bird calls. And you?"

He nodded and pointed toward the barn. "Over there, I detect a jeering, squawking blue jay and the cheeps of sparrows."

"You have a keen ear, Owen. Don't you love the

onomatopoeia of the chickadees' call from up in the eaves of the cottage? They're my favorite bird of all."

He chuckled again, enjoying the mirth dancing in her sparkling brown eyes. "Your favorite? Aye. Then I shall call you my wee chickadee."

"Well, *this* wee chickadee needs to check the chicken coop, milk the cow, and find Buoy. Our dog is really smart, but sometimes he runs off chasing a fox or rabbit and loses his way. He's been gone all night."

Owen scanned the property and clicked his tongue. "If he doesn't return soon, I'll help you look. At any rate, I'd be happy to assist you, for I simply can't be shirkin'. I must start earning my keep around here. The barn needs a fresh coat of whitewash, and the outhouse too. I don't recall ever painting, but I'm sure I can do it. Do you think your papa would allow me to be useful?"

Hopefully, he could work here until he figured out who he was and where he belonged. An indistinct niggling tickled a memory of a far different life. One of papers and proper clothing. Of stuffy rooms inside opulent buildings. Not this earthy existence.

He favored the latter.

"I'm sure he'd be grateful, Owen, at least until the temporary assistant keeper gets here. Will leaves early for work and doesn't return until dinnertime, so he's seldom available this summer. At the moment, though, I'd appreciate your help."

Before long, the morning's chores yielded five brown eggs and a bucket of fresh milk. As they left the barn with their finds, the watery horizon to the east revealed the river was coming alive with ships, boats, and waterfowl, and Buoy appeared, galloping up from the shoreline, sopping wet and smelling of fish.

Libby kept her distance as she lovingly scolded him, shaking a finger. "Where have you been all night? You had us worried. And no going into the house smelling like dead fish and wet dog."

As they climbed the steps to the porch, Buoy followed, his tail dragging behind him.

Libby pointed to the porch floor. "Stay."

While Libby prepared breakfast, Owen addressed Mr. Montonna. "May I please help around the lighthouse and earn my keep? Except for my scattered memory, I'm fit to do whatever you need, sir."

Over a plate of fresh eggs and toast, Papa agreed that whitewashing the buildings would be a good place for Owen to start. "I'd be much obliged. And polishing the brass would help too. Lives may depend on the light, so I like to keep it spit spot and sparkling. And we never know when the lighthouse inspector might pay us a call. 'Sides, I'd like to keep that award banner flying high for years to come."

After breakfast, Mr. Montonna handed him an old straw hat. "It'll be warm out there. Best cover those curls, and remember, you're still healing."

⁓

*A*fter a full day whitewashing the barn, Owen cocked his ear to beautiful music emanating from the keeper's house. The soft, sweet notes touched a longing, lonely cord within him. Suddenly, disenchantment pricked him like the sting of an angry hornet.

Why couldn't he remember? Something about that tune tickled his brain. A gray memory of that song muddled his thoughts. He strained to remember more than a vague woman playing it on a pianoforte when he was but a tyke. But no matter how hard he tried, clarity remained elusive.

With a weary sigh, he entered the house and found Libby at the parlor piano. She hummed the tune as her graceful hands danced along the keyboard. When she finished the moody melody, she began a livelier tune.

He knew it! He knew how to play that song!

His heart beat wildly, and without asking, he slipped onto the bench beside her and began playing the lower keys in perfect sync with her high notes.

Curiosity sparked in her eyes, but she laughed and kept on playing.

So did he.

When the song was done, Libby slipped her arm into his and hugged it. "How did you know? You play wonderfully."

He shrugged. "I just knew. When I heard the music, something clicked."

Her eyes twinkled from the reflection of the setting sun streaming through the window. "Perhaps we should play more together."

Behind them, Will cleared his throat loudly. "I think you should get dinner on the table, sister."

At the sound of Will's irritation, Owen sprung up from the bench and turned around. Libby froze.

Will stood in the doorway, arms folded, feet spread, as though he was ready for a fight. "It's time we had a talk, Owen. After dinner. Outside."

Libby huffed. "Wash your hands, gentlemen. Dinner will be on the table in a moment."

He and Will followed Libby into the kitchen where Mr. Montonna sat reading *The Old Farmer's Almanac*. "That was a lovely duet, you two. What's all the fuss about, Will?"

Libby scrambled to put the food on the already set table. Owen busied himself with washing his hands but listening for what Will might say. Why was he so angry with them? They were merely playing a song on the piano.

Will cleared his throat. "Nothing to worry about, Pa. I'll take care of it."

SUSAN G MATHIS

The pungent aroma of pan-fried fish blended with the scent of the warm yeast rolls and honey during what should have been a heavenly dinner. But the tension in the room and concern about the impending altercation with Will stole Owen's appetite, turning the few bites he managed into a loathsome meal. Try as he might, Owen couldn't understand what had Libby's brother so aggravated.

After enduring a supper of stilted and strained small talk, Papa excused himself to tend the light while Libby cleared the table.

Will opened the kitchen door. "Shall we have our talk now, Owen?"

Libby shrugged an apology as he stepped through the threshold behind Will.

Like a lamb to the slaughter.

CHAPTER 6

$\mathcal{L}$ibby washed the dishes as she listened to the indistinct murmurings of Owen and Will outside the window. She couldn't make out the words, but Will's tone was definitely impassioned, even outraged. Her brother had always been overprotective of her, but this was crossing a line. Owen didn't need this undue stress while he tried to find his memories. Perhaps it was time to set Will straight.

With every dish she washed, her frustration turned to exasperation that grew into fury. How dare he? Oh, that Alberta would return and talk sense into her husband!

"What's all this banging going on in here?"

Libby heaved a ragged sigh and almost dropped the plate she was washing as she turned to give her brother a piece of her mind.

With narrowed eyes, he scolded her again. "You're dripping greasy water all over the floor."

Libby grabbed a dish towel and wiped her hands, ready to let him have it. The back door slammed shut, and then the guest room door followed. Owen must be furious too.

For a moment, Libby bit her lip as she formulated what to

say. Her brother had always intimidated her, but she'd not back down. Not this time.

"I don't know what you think is going on here, but Owen is a good man. We've done nothing improper, I assure you, nor shall we. You have my word."

Her brother came within inches of her, staring through his spectacles down the bridge of his nose, his nostrils flaring, his eyes flashing. "I know men. You, missy, are playing with fire."

The ridiculousness of Will's anger birthed a giggle she failed to hold back. She swallowed a second giggle and forced a serious, strong tone. "Stop it, Will. I'm not playing with anything. I am a grown woman. You are my brother, and I love you, but you are seeing things that aren't there and stepping on grounds that aren't yours to walk."

"I'll involve Father if you don't stop flirting with that man. And he'll not be happy."

Will's threat shook her. When her brother got a burr under his saddle, there was no reasoning with him. Better to deflect and change the topic. She blew out a ragged breath to compose herself. "When will Alberta and Ralph return? They've been gone too long. I sure miss them."

Like popping a blister, Will instantly deflated. "So do I. I'm sorry, Libby, for being so forceful, but we don't know who this Owen fellow is. He could be trouble, and I don't want you hurt. Promise me you'll keep your distance."

Libby's anger dissipated too. "I will. But give me a little grace to be a grown woman and not your baby sister."

Will dipped his chin, but his eyes sparked sadness. "Goodnight, Libby."

In silence, Libby finished the dishes, then mopped up her spilled water before sweeping the floor. As she did, she washed and swept the residue of Will's displeasure out the door too. She'd not entertain it for another moment.

She glanced around the kitchen to be sure everything was

in order. When Alberta was home, she and her sister-in-law shared the cooking, cleaning, laundry, and sewing in a peaceful dance. She missed the camaraderie and wisdom of an older woman, especially now that Mama was gone. And she appreciated Alberta's way of calming down Will.

But what Libby enjoyed most of all was pickling and preserving their harvest with Alberta each autumn. The satisfaction of storing up their hard work for the cold and snowy winters was more fun than the holidays.

But tonight? She needed to work on long-neglected mending.

She moved into the parlor and began riffling through the overflowing basket of hand-sewn clothing. Except for Papa's keeper's uniform, the Montonna women made everything they wore. Mama had taught Libby well, and Alberta was an exceptional seamstress.

What should she work on first? A simple blouse needed a new button. A fluted skirt had a torn hem. Will's work shirt needed the cuff repaired. Baby Ralph's nightshirt and Papa's socks needed darning. She'd neglected the mending for too long.

At the bottom of the large wicker basket, Mama's chemise, a light cotton slip, and pantalets waited to be altered to fit Alberta or herself. Seeing them ripped a hole in her heart and tore her fractured emotions wide open again. She covered them with Papa's vest that needed its pocket repaired.

Yes, she wore her mama's hand-crocheted collars and brooch for her Sunday best. She even used her mama's fashionable hat, kid gloves, and low-heeled boots for special occasions. But Mama's undergarments? They were much too personal.

As Libby mended a frayed apron, the ticking of her mama's clock that had once provided her comfort no longer brought the peace she needed. Too many memories. Too many hurts.

A year ago, sorrow had skittered into her life on tiny mouse feet, rendering her heart a broken and trampled mess. Mama had betrayed her. Kept the essence of who Libby was from her all her life.

Worse, why did Mama make her promise to keep *the secret* their secret between only them? Did Papa know? Maybe he did, and it was a forbidden topic. At any rate, she didn't need to burden him.

Papa wore his own deep sorrow like an overcoat, protecting him from the loss of his wife. More than once, Libby had seen him caress the pillow on Mama's side of the bed, and often, other-worldly sobs followed. No, she couldn't add to that.

But why did Mama have to die before revealing who her real mama was? Perhaps, one day soon, Libby would break her promise, and Papa could answer her many questions and ease her burden.

It was as if she'd been delivered to the Montonnas' lighthouse in a basket—like Moses.

Adrift on the waves.

Alone in the world.

Like Owen.

Unbidden tears slipped from her eyes, blurring her handiwork. She heaved a deep, ragged sigh. She set her mending down, swiped at her tears, and moaned, "Why?"

"Can I help?" Owen stood in the doorway, a glass of water in his hand. How long had he seen her like this? "I was just getting a drink from the kitchen and heard you in here. What's wrong, Libby?"

She shook her head, dabbing her eyes with a handkerchief. "I miss my mama. She's been gone for more than a year."

Owen took a step toward her but quickly retreated two steps. "I'm sorry for your loss. I lost my brother when I was nine and Mother when I was ten."

With that confession, Owen's face turned ashen, and his

eyes widened, as if he'd been splashed with a bucket of ice-cold water. He raked a hand through his hair and sighed.

"I don't understand. How can I remember these things but not who I am?" He paused, swallowing hard. "I can't help but think of the Irish proverb that says, 'Even the truth may be bitter.' This is a bitter truth, indeed."

Libby crossed the room to join him and reached for his hand, but he clasped the water glass with both hands and took another step back. "I'm sorry for your loss, Owen, but don't you see? Your memories are returning faster and faster. I think, any moment now, they may return altogether. Wouldn't that be grand?"

He nodded, but he had erected an emotional wall between them.

She slipped her hands into her apron pockets. Had Will forbidden Owen to be near her? She'd ring his neck. "What did Will talk to you about? He sounded rather angry, but he's always been the protective big brother. He means no harm."

Owen shook his head as tears spiked his thick lashes, deepening their color and bidding her to be compassionate. "I've been a burden around here for far too long. It's time for me to be gone."

"Please don't go. Not now. Not until you're well."

He shrugged, turning toward the porch and grounds beyond. "Goodnight, Libby."

~

Owen shivered as the wind groaned through the trees swaying in the darkness. Fog slithered off the river, up the bank, and onto the Tibbetts Point Lighthouse grounds, bathing it in cool moisture and an eerie gloom. Soon it would rise to shroud everything in sight.

Owen took a gulp of his water and set the glass on the

porch railing. Even as the fog grew thicker by the minute, he determined to walk off his apprehension—or he'd not sleep a wink.

His uncharted life bothered him more by the day, but he also hurt for Libby. Underneath her confident demeanor lurked a childlike vulnerability and much pain. He'd guess that her hidden trials were deeper than the death of her mother. Much deeper.

A mist of sadness enveloped Owen as he stepped off the porch. He'd stay on the cement walkway that led from building to building. From the cottage to the outhouse. From the outhouse to the barn and chicken coup. The hundred or more feet of concrete maze made for safe navigation, if he stayed on it.

He had to think, and walking always helped.

This place had been a safe harbor from the storm within, but now what? Where would he go, and how would he live? And how could he leave Libby, whom he'd grown to admire, even cherish? He couldn't stay where Will had such hostility against him, and he needn't endanger the relationship between brother and sister.

No, he'd leave in the morning and find his way. Somehow.

"Is that you, Owen?" Mr. Montonna's question reverberated down through the tower and out the door as he passed by it. "Could you please lend a hand?"

He stepped into the tower. "Yes, sir. Be right up."

Owen climbed the stairs, his heart beating faster with each echoing step. Was Mr. Montonna in danger? Hurt? His tone didn't sound urgent or worried.

When he reached the top, the keeper snapped an appreciative glance his way. "Thanks for coming. I had thought of waking Will to lend his eyes, but he's been in such a foul mood of late. I expect he misses his wife and son more than he'd admit. When I saw you pacing the grounds though a break in the fog, I thought maybe you could fill in for him instead."

Owen saluted him. "At your service, sir. How can I help? I'll do anything you need."

Mr. Montonna scanned the landscape for a moment before answering. "These foggy nights are the most dangerous time of all for sailing, especially for the freighters and steamers, but also for those foolish enough to navigate the fog in smaller boats. An extra pair of eyes and someone to talk to on such a night is a mighty big help."

Owen scanned the dark night. "Aye. I'd be happy to assist. I believe I've been on such foggy waters, and they are terrifying. I've also been in the city during fog with blinding automobile lights and honking horns, and all of that chaos troubles me. I must say, I fancy the peace and quiet here."

"You live in a city? What city?"

"I don't know. Memories bounce around my brain and out of my mouth like marbles. I don't know where they come from or if they are true or not, and that bothers me more than a traffic jam or a foggy night." He sighed, weary of the uncertainties bombarding him.

Mr. Montonna handed him a cup of coffee. "This may prove a long night for you. Are you up for it? I can always call Will or Libby to help."

"Oh, sir, please. I want to help. Besides, Libby seems very sad tonight, and, well...she misses her mother."

Should he reveal such grief to her papa?

Mr. Montonna nodded. "Yes, Libby and her mother were very close. Libby went to the local one-room schoolhouse until grade eight, but then her mama taught her beyond that. Her mother was a well-educated, upper-class woman who gave it all up for me. But she loved it here, and we had a wonderful marriage. I expect my daughter will hurt for a long while."

The lightkeeper's pain ran deep too. How could he cheer

the man? "An Irish blessing comes to mind—'May you never forget what is worth remembering, nor ever remember what is best forgotten.' And don't ask me how I recall that and not my surname or from where I came, for I have no idea."

Mr. Montonna chuckled. "Don't fret. Time will sort things out. Every person has a wound. Some you can see. Others are hidden deep in the recesses of one's heart or mind. Only hope and love can bring it out into the light where it can be healed. And more than not, a lot of patience."

"Thank you for that."

But what if he never discovered his heritage, his family, the essence of who he really was? Without it, how could he move forward? He shoved his hands in his pockets and whispered a prayer for divine revelation.

The lightkeeper handed him an empty can. "We need a full supply of kerosene for the night, and I haven't brought up enough of it for fog like this. Would you be a good lad and fetch it, please?"

"Aye. I'll be right back."

He descended the tower and fetched kerosene from the oil house feet from the lighthouse. He carried one of the heavy copper pitchers of kerosene up the winding metal stairs, grabbing hold of the pipe handrail for balance as the mesh metal stairs rumbled under his feet. How did Mr. Montonna accomplish this difficult task night after night?

After ascending the first ladder, he reached the near-vertical ladder that led to the open hatch door and hoisted the can up to the lightkeeper. "Aye, here's the fuel. Might you be needing more?"

The lightkeeper took the fuel from Owen. "Thank you. One more should do the trick for tonight. But perhaps two spares would ensure the light will shine brightly if this fog decides to stay around in the morning."

"Your wish is my command, captain." As Owen repeated the process twice more, his hair and clothing grew wet from sweat and the moist air. Truly, the lightkeeper's was no easy life.

Once Owen finished the task, he joined Mr. Montonna in scanning the dark and murky river. "When is your assistant keeper coming, sir? I should vacate his quarters before that, so I'm thinking that tomorrow might be a good time to be on my way."

The lightkeeper scanned the river through his binoculars one more time before searching Owen's face. "The fellow I hired as my temporary assistant—at my own expense, mind you—is Leonard Bruner. He'll do a lot of the yard work, painting, and such that you have been doing—for which I thank you very much. But he isn't due for another two weeks, so there's no need to hurry off. I've spoken to the board about bringing Will on next year as the permanent assistant keeper and training him to take over for me some day, but Congress has to approve the added personnel, and they move slower than a glacier."

"Does the lightkeeper's position usually transfer from father to son?"

"At times." Mr. Montonna shrugged. "And now and then, the wife or daughter, though that is rare. Maybe one day, things will be more equitable."

Owen leaned against the wall. "One day, perhaps. This job seems to be unceasing. Tell me more about what you do, please."

Libby's father chuckled. "Well now, besides keeping the light through the night, we must maintain daily reports of weather, river traffic, and much more. Light keeping is more of a calling than a job, I believe. Did you know that a lightkeeper is oftentimes called a wickie? It refers to our job of trimming the wicks. We're also called a steward or custodian, and our motto is 'maintain.' Maintain what, you ask? Oh, everything on the property. The keeper is paid for an eight-hour day, but the work takes much more time than that."

Owen rubbed his chin. "And you maintain the buildings, lawn, and shoreline too? And you grow your own food and keep animals?"

Mr. Montonna continued to survey the darkness while answering. "Keepers are given two hundred pounds of pork, one hundred pounds of beef, and also an allotment of beans or peas each year as part of our salary. We supplement that by raising chickens, keeping a milk cow, and growing a garden. Thankfully, the womenfolk usually take on those jobs, so I can focus on the other work. An assistant keeper, even a temporary one, will be helpful, as you are, son. But by far, our most important duty is keeping the light and protecting those on the water." Mr. Montonna tossed him a pointed gaze. "And sometimes helping a fellow traveler in need is a keeper's priority too."

Humbled by his kindness, Owen smiled. "I commend you, sir, and thank you for keeping us all safe, especially me. I must admit, I never really thought about the importance of a lighthouse keeper before now. I'd be honored to assist you in anything you need as long as I'm here."

Mr. Montonna nodded his appreciation, and for the next few hours, he taught Owen how to clean the lens and surrounding glass prisms. Then he set him to polish the brass while he washed the windows. "I once heard that the past is a lighthouse, not a port. I suppose we all must choose to move beyond our past and not get stuck there."

"But what if the past is too hazy for us to see? How can I move on when I don't know where I'm moving from?"

Mr. Montonna scratched his chin. "Well now, that is a pickle. But until you remember, you must stay with us. Even if the assistant keeper comes before you're well, you can bed down in the barn until you know where to go. I shan't have you traipsing out into the unknown, and that's final."

But what about Will?

And Libby?

CHAPTER 7

The next morning, Libby swiped at a stray lock of hair as she stoked the stove. Retrieving the kettle from the back burner, she poured the boiling water into her mama's teapot. Papa, Will, and Owen would be ready for breakfast soon.

She blew out a breath, rolling her eyes at her incessant thoughts of the man who'd come into her life barely a month ago. She'd dreamed of Owen again last night, and though she didn't really want those dreams to end, with the arrival of Leonard, he would be leaving soon.

Forever.

Her heart dropped to her feet as she blinked back unbidden tears. Who could help her sort out these thoughts?

Yes, she'd talked with Connie about her deepening feelings toward Owen. But being a confirmed spinster and a too-logical nurse, Connie had declared it a mere puppy-love crush and dismissed her feelings as inconsequential.

Libby sighed, longing to understand these new emotions. Longing to know what to do with them. If only Mama were here. Before the secret.

The morning sunlight trickled through the curtains, casting shadows that danced on the plank floors. She and Owen had shared poetry and long walks, merriment and dreams, chores and meals. His presence had been a sweet reprieve from the grief and heartache that had haunted her for over a year. How could she face the days ahead without him?

Papa's presence interrupted her musings. "Good morning, daughter. It's only you, me, and Owen for breakfast. Will left early to meet Alberta at the Clayton train station. They came on the overnight, so they should be back sometime this morning."

She handed him a cup of coffee and planted a kiss on his cheek. "Finally. I have missed them so, and I'm sure baby Ralph has grown like a weed."

He indicated his thanks and chuckled heartily. "They do at that age. You sure did. I remember when you were that small. One day, you were sitting on the floor playing with a ball of yarn. Then, without ever crawling, you stood and took your first steps. Mama and I marveled at your tenacity and enjoyed every moment of your growth. What a precocious child you were!"

An apple-sized lump threatened to cut off her air. She slipped the biscuits from the oven and turned toward the door. "I'll be right back."

She hurried outside and headed toward the outhouse. How old was she when her birth mother abandoned her? Mama hadn't said. So many unknowns pricked and poked at her heart, piercing it with pain.

How she longed to demand that Papa tell her everything. But not yet. His heart still hurt, too, and she'd not add to that.

Will wouldn't help. He was only five when she came along. Who could help her carry this heavy burden?

She put her hand on the outhouse handle just as Owen exited it. "Gracious! Sorry. I didn't know you were in there." Her face flamed as if too close to the fire. She put her hands on her cheeks to both hide and cool them.

Owen laughed, waving off her concerns. "How were you to know? Aye, top of the morning, my sweet chickadee. Did you hear the birds chirping this morning? They made me think of you and thank God for all your kindness and care. Truly, Libby, you've been a godsend over this past month, and I'm beholden to you. I've enjoyed every moment we've shared together, and I'm pleased to say that your father has urged me to stay a little longer."

Libby sucked in a breath. "I'm so glad, Owen, but if you'll excuse me, I must hurry back to get breakfast on the table."

He nodded as she scurried into the outhouse. The intensity of his words conveyed a passion that both frightened and thrilled her. His charm left her discombobulated. Disoriented. Confused. And he was staying? The humid day left dampness on her neck, her bodice, her legs. Or was it his words?

She abandoned her concerns for the time being and returned to the kitchen, where Papa and Owen chatted and sipped coffee.

Papa pointed to the newspaper article. "How did Milton Hershey start the Hershey Chocolate Company and how did Coca-Cola find a way to bottle its drink in the middle of this depression?"

Owen shrugged. "Perhaps they believe the Panic of 1893 is soon to pass? Though it has affected every area of the economy and caused much distress in the political arena, perhaps there were businessmen unfettered by loss?"

Libby added the pot of tea, a bowl of berries, and a plate of biscuits to the table. "How do you know all this, Owen? Your knowledge of the world astounds me."

Her papa raised an eyebrow, but she ignored it.

Owen slathered a biscuit with honey before answering. "I read your papa's papers at night. They are quite informative."

Papa sipped his coffee. "Did you read about the Pullman strike last month? Three thousand workers of the Pullman Palace Car Company went on strike."

"Aye. I believe Pullman has an entire city of workers in Illinois."

Papa pointed a finger toward the northeast. "Right you are, and he also owns one of the Thousand Islands downriver from here. He named it Pullman Island. Back in '72, President Grant came to visit, and that started the whole bruhaha of the rich and famous scooping up the islands in the region. The entire Thousand Islands area hasn't been the same since."

Libby joined the men at the table and poured a cup of tea. "Did you read about the Canadian passenger steamer *Ocean* that collided with the American barge Kent near the Sister's Island Lighthouse last month? The keeper's family rescued all but two of the *Ocean's* deckhands before both vessels sank."

Owen blanched. "I hadn't read that. A shipwreck is a terrible thing."

A baby's wail drew their notice as Alberta walked through the door. Will followed close behind, carrying a case and dragging the crying toddler.

Libby jumped up and ran to her sister-in-law, taking an overnight case from her and setting it on the counter. "Gracious! You're home. I thought you weren't coming until later."

Alberta wrapped her in a warm embrace before picking up Ralph and handing him to her.

"He's walking? When did that happen?"

Libby grabbed a cloth and wiped the tears from the child's eyes. Then she snuggled her nephew, but he squirmed to be free. Had he forgotten her?

Alberta *tsk*ed. "Don't mind him. Ever since Ralph took to his feet two weeks ago, he refuses to be held by anyone. Unless he's asleep or eating, he's on the move. I'm just glad he slept through most of the train trip."

Libby set the child down, and he promptly toddled to the open cupboard, grabbed a pot, and began banging on it. She giggled at his antics.

"And he has two new teeth? So much happens in a month of babyhood."

Alberta leaned in and whispered, "I hear a lot has happened here too?" Her sister-in-law raised an eyebrow and glanced at Owen, a knowing glimmer in her brown eyes.

Owen and Papa stared at them.

Libby clucked her tongue. "I'm sorry. This is Owen, our recovering sea-farer."

Alberta gave him a little curtsey, acknowledging him with a soft smile. "Welcome to our home. I hope you've been properly cared for. And hello, Papa. I've missed you."

She kissed Papa's cheek, and he hugged her back. "Welcome home. Now, if you'll excuse me, I need a few hours of sleep. Then I want to play with this little man." Papa scooped Ralph into a bear hug, but the boy pushed away and squirmed until he set him down. "What have you been feeding this child? He must have gained five pounds."

Alberta and Will laughed together. Will answered him. "I agree. I barely knew him."

Owen cleared his throat, clearly uncomfortable with the intimate family discussion. "I'll check the garden. Rabbits have been nibbling on the tender plants, and I'm determined to find their burrow and send them packing. Nice to meet you, Mrs. Montonna. If you'll excuse me."

Libby followed Owen to the porch. "I'll join you soon."

"Aye. Take your time." He winked, sending a warm jolt through her.

What was a girl to do?

When she returned to the kitchen, only Alberta remained. She'd already partially cleared the table.

Alberta grabbed her hand and tittered. "Come. Let's have tea and talk. I want to know...everything."

"What is that grin about? What did my brother say? I hope he's not telling tales. I'll skin him alive."

"Hah! I don't need Will's opinions. I can see with my own two eyes. You're smitten, girl. And so is your stranger."

The tiny hairs on the back of Libby's neck stood up. Was it that obvious? Her ire rose to the muscles in her jaw. She clenched them tight. "You've been here five minutes and you know all that? What did Will tell you?"

"Calm down. You two are ridiculous. He's so over-protective, I want to throw him in the river to cool him off. You're so defensive, I might have you join him. Your brother is concerned, that's all." Alberta took a sip of her tea as if giving herself time to formulate her next words.

Libby had words of her own. "Owen has been nothing but honorable, and I have done nothing wrong. Will is not my keeper."

Alberta reached across the table and took her hands. "Please be careful. He's a stranger. You don't even know who he is, and neither does he."

Libby scoffed. "And who am I? Perhaps we're both strangers."

Perhaps that was all too true.

～

*O*wen assisted Libby as she quickly gathered the laundry from the line and brought it inside when the afternoon wind kicked up angry whitecaps on the water and started battering the clean wash. Thunderheads grew enormous, moving closer by the moment. The wind howled as rain sprinkled and then pelted them.

Libby dropped the wicker laundry basket inside the house

and grabbed his hand. "Come with me. Before the gale takes hold."

She tugged him to the tower, and he followed her up the staircase. Ten steps up, she stopped suddenly, her eyes glistening with exhilaration. "You simply must experience a thunderstorm from high atop the tower. It's terrifying, mesmerizing, and thrilling all at the same time. You'll never forget it. Hurry."

Never forget? He'd never forget *her*—that much he knew.

He climbed the stairs, recalling numerous precious moments with her. Libby had shared her love of the gardens, and it seemed as though she could coax the flowers to bloom a soft winter white, buttery yellow, enchanting crimson, brilliant orange, deep velvety violet, and soft lilac that filled the air with a glorious perfume no man could capture in a bottle. She'd even created a wee fairyland fit for a queen of fairies—an intricate miniature garden with fossils and feathers and moss and tiny bark huts. She'd taught the squirrels and chipmunks to eat from her hand and the hummingbirds and butterflies to alight on her outstretched finger.

Could he truly love a woman so earthy and socially insignificant?

He did.

Libby stopped on the second landing, and he almost bumped into her. His gaze slipped to her luscious lips, and he wet his own. Then he drew her near and wrapped his arms around her tiny waist. Like the sizzle of energy during an electrical storm, his touch caused her to quiver under his touch.

What was he doing?

He'd send her fleeing, and her brother and father would accost him if they saw. He dropped his arms to his side and shoved his hands deep into his pockets. Then he tipped his head, and his brow arched in apology, though his ragged breath revealed his errant desire.

"Forgive me. I lost myself in your charms. Shall we ascend?"

There was nothing coy or seductive about Libby. She was pure and innocent. Her eyes flashed, but then she turned and silently climbed the remaining ladders with much less gusto. She disappeared through the hatch without a word.

How could he face her after that bumbling breach of etiquette? What a buffoon!

A flash of lightning burst through the hatch door, beckoning him upward. Though it was not yet sunset, the lightkeeper already stood at his station, lamp lit, ready to help any boaters in peril.

When Owen entered the warm watch room, neither Mr. Montonna nor Libby acknowledged him. The lightkeeper intently searched the churning river with his binoculars, while Libby silently stared into the storm. Would Libby tell her papa of his shenanigans? If so, he might be sent away this very night. He had to redeem himself somehow.

"How may I help, sir?"

The lightkeeper looked at him and blinked, then handed him a second pair of binoculars. "Sorry, Owen. I was concentrating on the river. This looks to be a humdinger of a gale. Stay and keep watch with me, if you'd like."

As the beam of light rotated 'round and 'round, the tempest increased. Turbulent clouds, pelting rain, and massive swells created a war on the water. Thunder pummeled the air, groaning in agreement with his thoughts and feelings.

Why did he lose control and almost kiss her? He shouldn't have. He wanted to.

Rain pelted the window and roof, and soon the storm grew even angrier, roaring its fury. He prayed that every boater had already taken shelter, that there would be no casualties.

Cautiously, Owen slipped close to Libby and whispered, "I'm sorry."

She turned and stared into his face for a moment, her closed lips trembling, her eyes misty. "It's okay."

But was it? Had he imagined the attraction between them? Did she think he was trying to take advantage of her humble station in life?

They couldn't talk more about it in her papa's presence, even with the sound of wind, rain, and thunder echoing loudly through the watch room. Besides, they, too, were on duty.

At a burst of lightning followed by a thunderclap that shook the tower, Libby jumped and then slowly blew out a breath and raised her chin as if gathering her courage. "That was a doozy."

Mr. Montonna spoke from behind his binoculars. "These summer storms are often like this, Owen. One minute, gentle and peaceful. The next, deadly. Being up in the tower can be frightening, but the beauty of it supersedes the terror, I think."

"I agree," Owen and Libby said in unison.

The three of them burst into laughter, dispelling the tension of the moment—and moments past.

When Libby accidentally brushed a hand on his forearm, he jerked away as though he were struck by lightning. Yet her touch was so slight that it reminded him of a fairy's whose sole aim was to coax an unwelcome and uncontrollable quiver from deep inside him.

Nonsense. Utter, aggravating nonsense.

Why would such a fair lass be interested in a man who didn't even know who he was?

The assistant keeper would be here in three days, and though Mr. Montonna had offered Owen shelter in the barn, perhaps he should leave and spare everyone the drama of their growing affection. But where would he go? Where did he belong?

"Owen? Can you not hear me over this gale?"

Blathers! The lightkeeper was almost shouting to him.

"Sir? Sorry. What did you say?"

Mr. Montonna pointed to the large copper pitcher Owen had used before to carry the oil to fill the lamp. "Could you fetch another round of oil, please? I believe this is going to be a long night."

"Aye, sir, and I shall watch through the night with you, if you'd like. A second pair of eyes can't hurt."

"I'd appreciate that, son." Mr. Montonna turned to his daughter. "Libby, why don't you go down and be with Alberta? You know how she fears these storms, and I imagine the baby won't enjoy the thunder either."

Libby shook her head. "Will's with them. I'd rather stay here and help keep watch."

The lightkeeper waved his arm toward the hatch door. "Go on, now. I want to talk with Owen. Man to man."

Libby's eyes grew alarmed, but she obeyed. "Goodnight, Papa. Owen."

Owen picked up the pitcher and followed her. "I'll be right back with more oil, sir."

Once Owen caught up with Libby on the first landing, he gently took her hand. "Wait. Please. I must beg your forgiveness and ask if you might tell your father of my error. Should I?"

Libby sighed, her eyes brimming with tears. "No, and there's nothing to forgive, Owen. I must confess, I feel the same inclination toward you. That's why I was upset. But it's no use. You'll soon be leaving, and I'll remain here. Moreover, once you gain your memories back and discover your former life that I expect is far grander than this, I will be of no consequence. This magical time will be a fading memory, and you'll go on with your life. So will I. Goodnight, sir."

As if she had sliced his heart and cut it out of his chest, a deep ache kept him from speaking out. From breathing, even. She'd rejected him, and that was that.

She scurried down the steps like a rabbit running from a fox. Even in the darkness, she was sure of foot and fled into the storm before he could make it to the next landing. He stopped and he swallowed a sob. "Oh God! What have I done?"

He trudged down the remaining stairs to the service room and poked his head out the door to see Libby retreating through the back door of the house. Once he filled the copper pitcher, he slogged back up to the light, his hopes dashed like a skiff on the rocks.

Upon Owen's return to the small watch room, Mr. Montonna stood waiting. "Thank you, Owen. Did Libby get back to the house all right?"

"She did. Shall I fill the oil?"

The lightkeeper grinned, but it held sadness within it. "I'm not blind, son. You have eyes for my daughter, and she is smitten with you. Please don't encourage it. You still don't know who you are, and I don't want Libby hurt. She's an innocent and gentle soul."

Owen sighed. "Aye. I understand, Mr. Montonna."

But what about *his* soul?

CHAPTER 8

*L*ibby slept little, cried much, brooded more. She had to talk to someone, or she'd burst. The burden of her mama's secret—*her secret*—had become too much to bear, especially after piling on the confusing sentiments of her growing feelings and the uncertainties about Owen and his past.

As she entered the kitchen, Alberta hummed quietly, kneading the bread. Alone. Perhaps she could offer solace?

Alberta, only a few years older than her own twenty years, had married Will a little over a year ago. She returned from the honeymoon, moved into the Tibbetts' cottage, promptly found out she was with child, and settled into life at Tibbetts Point Lighthouse. Libby and Alberta became fast friends.

Her brother's wife became the sister Libby had always wanted, and they danced around their daily chores like professional ballerinas. They rarely disagreed, but when they did, Will was almost always the cause.

"Good morning, sister. May I help?"

Alberta nodded, tore a generous piece of dough from her lump, and set it on the breadboard. She studied Libby for a moment. "I see you've sewn a new dress while I was gone. It's very nice, I must say. I just made tea. Have a cup before you get your hands sticky."

Libby assessed her light calico day dress, smoothing the full skirt she'd carefully hemmed to brush the tops of her shoes. Her apron covered most of her dress and coordinated nicely.

Instead of helping with the bread, Libby plopped down in a chair, stalling for time as she formulated her thoughts into words. Her sewing certainly wasn't what she wanted to talk about, and she'd come to help, not sit like a useless ball of clay.

Alberta eyed her suspiciously but continued to knead the dough. "Papa's asleep, and Ralph is napping. Will took Owen into town. It's only us women here. Talk to me, Libby. I see you're vexed."

Libby swiped the hair from her face. Nothing felt right. "I'm sorry. I miss Mama's shepherd pie and stews. I miss her."

Alberta grabbed both pieces of dough and dropped them into a bowl, covering it with a towel. She scooted a chair closer to Libby's, sat, and took her hand. "I miss your mother too. But I'm sure you miss her even more. You two were so close. Shall I make her shepherd's pie tonight? Would that help?"

Tears teased the back of Libby's eyelids until she could no longer hold back the flood. They trickled down her cheeks, one or two at a time at first, and then they came faster and faster, as though a dam had burst. Sobs followed, so her sister-in-law wrapped her in her arms and rubbed her back. For several minutes, Libby could say nothing. She simply wept.

It was the first time since the funeral she'd let any of it out. She'd imprisoned her pain behind a high, secure wall, carefully plastering on a fake smile and calm demeanor when needed, all the while feeling like a fraud. She'd successfully kept a stiff upper lip, as her mama had called it. But it all came tumbling down in this one brief moment, and now what was she to do?

She felt like a fool. A child. A weak young woman at best. She could no longer hide her pain.

Libby wiped her tears, blew her nose in her hanky, and let out a deep, anguished sigh. "I've lost my way. I no longer know who I am." Her words came out choppy and whiny.

Alberta patted her hand and poured the tea before responding. When she did, her tone held an almost motherly compassion. "Drink this. It'll soothe your frayed nerves. I think it's normal to feel a bit cattywampus for a while after we lose someone dear to us. Love is what makes us feel fully alive, so when someone we love departs, we tend to question our own existence." She paused, tilting her head. "But is that really what is creating this angst? Your mother has been gone for over a year. Could your unease be coming from the presence of a certain handsome stranger who has captured your thoughts and feelings? Could Owen be the actual cause of questioning your heart and life?"

Libby blinked. Might Alberta be right? Was Owen the reason for this war within her and not her mama's secret that had become her own? Oh, how confusing love and emotions and relationships could be! How much should she reveal about her feelings for Owen?

"Owen is a good man, Alberta, and I've enjoyed his company ever so much. He likes poetry and nature, as I do. We have laughed and shared deep thoughts. And he has been so helpful this past month while you were gone, doing chores and assisting Papa and me with the work around here. Will has never approved of him, but Owen has brought me much joy."

Alberta stared at the ceiling for a moment before looking straight into Libby's eyes until she squirmed under her sister-in-law's gaze.

"But Owen still doesn't know who he is. He might be anyone, Libby. A married sailor from Europe. An explorer gone awry. A father with a brood of young ones. And no, from what little I know of him, I don't believe he is a pirate or a scallywag, as Will might surmise. Still, he is a stranger in this strange land, and he doesn't belong here."

A long, shaky groan slipped from Libby's lips. "And where do I belong? Who am I?"

Alberta smoothed Libby's hair with a gentle hand. "You're a Montonna, daughter of a fine and upstanding lightkeeper, my sister, and a child of God."

Libby stared at her through tear-stained eyes. Should she break her promise to keep the secret? Her mama had almost kept it to the grave, but then she revealed it with her last breath and made her daughter promise to keep it a secret to her dying days. From everyone. Yet Libby was so utterly tired of carrying it alone, so overly burdened by holding onto it. That secret had become a poison that tainted her very soul, a ghost that haunted her dreams, a knife that pricked her heart.

She hated secrets. Always had.

When her school chums whispered secrets during recess, she avoided being a part of it. When Connie told her that her mama was having another baby but that she had to keep it a secret, the worry over not spilling the beans to her own mama kept her awake night after night.

Libby was about ten when she saw the village women whisper to one another and look her way, but she never knew why. She'd known they were sharing secrets. About her.

Now, she wondered, did they know *her secret*?

Through the years, she had heard bits and pieces of gossip. As she shopped at the general store, overhearing Mrs. Brownly tell her mother-in-law that the lightkeeper's daughter was a foundling. Mrs. Reston calling her a waif to another lady during a church picnic.

She'd dismissed it all as idle gossip and silly chatter. When she'd mentioned the comments to Mama, she'd agreed.

Then, when Libby was about fourteen, she walked in on a

conversation between her mama and the minister, and they both turned crimson red. A discussion about *her*.

Did the minister know?

Did Alberta know? Did Will?

Ralph's cry echoed down the steps, beckoning Alberta to his care, so her sister-in-law excused herself, leaving Libby to wallow in her anxious thoughts.

How could she talk with her sister-in-law and not have Will's opinions influence her? If she divulged her secret, what would Will think? Would Papa be hurt that she didn't talk to him first?

Will's voice boomed in the hallway. "We're home, and we found a straggler on the road."

He stepped into the kitchen carrying the basket of goods he'd been sent to buy, followed by Owen carrying a crate of supplies for the light. Behind them stood a tall, lanky young man who appeared to be even younger than herself. He had stiff, wiry brown hair that stuck up in all directions, his deep-set eyes the color of charcoal. They held a touch of sadness in them, as if a fire had burned out on a cold, dark night. His square jaw was clean shaven, but he had a silly hint of a beard under his mouth that looked like a door-knocker.

Why had Papa hired such a boy to help him? Surely, she could do better work than he.

He stopped in the doorway and stared at her, a frown so evident she checked to see if she had drooled or had something on her face.

Libby needed to break the awkward silence. Fast. "And who is this?"

Will chuckled, setting the basket on the table. "Leonard Bruner, the temporary assistant Father hired. He's arrived two days earlier than we had planned, mind you. We found him walking along the shore road, so we picked him up."

Libby stood and curtsied, but she glanced at Owen, who

looked none too happy. "Welcome." She pasted on a smile as best she could, but her tone was flat. "Papa will be pleased."

Leonard bobbed his head but didn't return her smile. "Thank you. Where shall I put my things?"

Owen cleared his throat. His face held a frown. No. More like simmering exasperation. His blue eyes turned icy. "Since you're early, I haven't cleared out of *your* room. But as soon as I deliver these supplies to the tower, I'll move out of the quarters and into the barn until I figure out where to go."

His tone confirmed Libby's assessment of the man. Trouble already brewed between them.

An uncomfortable silence followed until Alberta joined them with Ralph on her hip. "And who is this?"

Will reintroduced Leonard to his wife and son, but the assistant keeper barely acknowledged either of them. Who was this man who would now be living under the same roof, displacing Owen, and bringing with him a mood so foreboding that her own fretfulness seemed insignificant?

And now, how much longer would she have to stow her secrets?

Could she?

≈

Owen seethed at what he had heard in the hardware store. How dare that woman talk about him—and worse, about Libby—as though she knew a dirty little secret about them and had the inside scoop on imagined trespasses that didn't exist.

Blathers! He'd never even seen that woman before, so for her to spread such malicious and completely untrue gossip sent his temper to smolder, finally flaming into a fire that refused to be quenched. His pulse had raced and palms had sweated, and a giant ball of twine had filled his throat. It was all he could do to hold his tongue and not lash out at her, even as Will had joined the women for a friendly chat about the Sunday sermon.

That nasty woman even had the nerve to call Libby a foundling and accused her of walking alone, arm in arm, with an interloper who had tarried too long at the lighthouse.

That interloper was him!

When the woman had glanced his way and lowered her voice, it was difficult to hear anything else she'd said to the shop owner's wife. But he'd heard enough. Enough to flee the store and stew until Will came out.

What else were people in the village saying about Libby—because of him? Surely, it was high time to leave and let Libby and her family live in peace.

Still, something about this scrappy Leonard fellow bothered Owen. He felt it deep in his bones. Saw it in the assistant keeper's dark eyes. Something mysterious, secretive. And the lad confirmed it the moment he met Libby and stared at her all too intensely.

Owen shook off the frustration surging through his veins. He hurried to the service room and deposited the crate between a wooden box of wicks and tools, and another crate of slickers used in foul weather. Buzzing bugs, pesty gnats, and irritating mosquitoes flew around him as if to prod his already disturbed state to another level.

He swatted his way back to the house to pack up the few things he'd accumulated during his six weeks of recuperation. Two sets of clothes Will had donated and that Libby had perfectly altered for him. An ancient shaving set Mr. Montonna bequeathed him. An old straw hat that was once Libby's mother's. The pocket watch that a boy had found on the shore, and a bar of soap. That was all.

As he took the pile of belongings to the barn, he fumed about the buggy ride back to Tibbetts Point. Leonard hadn't asked Will about the assistant keeper's duties. He didn't even ask about the lighthouse or about his superior, Mr. Montonna. He interrogated Will about his sister. How old was she? How did she like living so far from the village?

This young spit of a thing was far too interested in his Libby. How could he leave her alone with Leonard in the same house?

And moreover, Libby had been crying when they walked in. Her blotchy cheeks and red eyes betrayed her, and the half smile she'd pasted on to introduce herself didn't raise to her eyes. Why?

So many unanswered, perplexing questions.

He entered the barn and set his things on a dusty, rough-hewn wooden shelf. The pungent smell of hay and animals accosted his nose. He examined the stalls, the milking pen, and the upper loft where he would sleep. It'd be warm and comfortable enough for now. Aye, he'd sleep in the barn with the cows and the horse and goats until he knew she was safe.

If it took a lifetime.

Truth was, he didn't want to leave this special piece of the world—or Libby. He'd experienced peace and joy and companionship as he'd never known before. At least none he could remember.

He sighed, forcing down his dismay as he climbed down the loft ladder and brushed bits of straw from his pants.

When would his memories finally and fully return? And when they did, what might change?

"Are you in here, Owen? Can you help me in the garden, please?"

Libby rounded the corner, almost colliding with him at the barn door with Buoy on her heels. The dog trotted up to him and rubbed against his leg, begging for a scratch behind his ears. He didn't disappoint the amiable creature, stalling for a moment to gather his wits and set aside his jitters.

He cleared his throat. "Aye, I'd be happy to help, my lovely chickadee, but I weeded it yesterday, so it should be in good order."

Libby shook her head, her floppy hat teetering on her head. "Varmints have attacked the tomatoes, cucumbers, beans, and peppers again. If they keep this up, we'll have no produce to can for the winter. What is ravaging them, do you suppose?"

He raised his palms to the sky. "Who knows? Perhaps rabbits, but they could also be raccoons or squirrels."

He followed Libby to the garden on the other side of the barn. Sure enough, many of the tender young plants had been chewed. "Couldn't be deer—no prints. Perhaps I shall sleep out here tonight and discover the culprits."

Libby covered her mouth and giggled, but then she quickly sobered, surprise etching her pretty face. "When I found you on the shore, your clothing suggested an upper-class status. But here you are now, an expert on varmints. And planning to sleep under the stars? I daresay you are a man of mystery, and I fear I shall miss you terribly when you leave."

Sadness and foreboding nibbled at him like the critters attacking the garden. He had to shake it off, or he'd succumb to their taunts.

He bent down, plucked a dandelion, and handed it to her. "My mother always said that when you look at a dandelion, you can see either a hundred weeds or a hundred wishes. I must admit my feelings for you have blossomed from weeds into wishes, but what of them? I shall soon be gone, and they will come to naught."

Libby clutched the weed to her chest and closed her eyes. "Then I shall wish for a million miracles."

He willed confidence to warm his tone. "And I shall join you, fair lass. But please, I must ask you a favor."

Libby batted her eyelashes, a soft smile setting his heart to quiver. "Anything, Owen."

His jaw tensed as he measured his words. "Please be careful

around Leonard, my sweet lass. There's a dark mystery about him, and he unsettles me. I don't know why, but he does."

Libby's brows furrowed, and she pursed her lips. "Papa's friend said his nephew, Leonard, was a hard worker and in desperate need of work, so Papa took Mr. Klint's advice and hired him for the summer. Still, Leonard does seem rather mysterious. Perhaps Papa will learn his story."

"I hope so, and I pray it's nothing to be concerned about. Yet he asked too many questions about you on the way home for my peace of mind."

A slight smirk teased her lips. "Are...are you jealous? You needn't be."

Owen felt the blood rise to his neck. How dare she accuse him of jealousy, like some silly schoolboy? "That's a rather scrappy thing to say, Miss Montonna. Forewarned is forearmed. Now if you'll excuse me, I have things to do."

With that, he fled to the barn. But he tripped over Buoy, skinning his hands and bruising his knees even more than his pride.

CHAPTER 9

The simple, well-worn parlor furniture still retained a quiet elegance. A brocade settee in blue. Two matching chairs. Papa's desk. A bookshelf filled with books. Mama's piano. Heavy drapes, currently opened to let in the sunshine and fresh air.

Libby sat at the keeper's desk recording the weather. She ran her hand over the thick logbook that the lighthouse board demanded be filled out daily. They required the keepers to journal not only the weather conditions but also repairs, upkeep, station inspections, rescues, supplies used, duties completed, and visitors, as well as any personal changes—from being ill to losing Mama.

She'd been helping her father with the task ever since he'd become lightkeeper nine years ago, and she thoroughly enjoyed it. On the day Papa became lightkeeper, he said, "Would you do me the honor of keeping the ledger, daughter? You have such perfect penmanship. Every letter is as beautiful as you, and my handwriting is as scratchy as an old rooster's."

She brightened at the memory of the compliment, picked

up her pen, dipped it into the inkwell, and faithfully recorded the weather patterns in the journal.

The stormy weather over the past three days has passed. Windy, warm, clear. Slight waves to a little choppy. Temperature a pleasant 76 degrees. The July fourth evening celebration should be lovely.

Leonard stomped into the room. "Please stop. You needn't pen another thing. Your father showed me the ledger, so I'll assume that job now, miss." The insistence in his voice startled her as he reached out to take the pen from her, but she held it tightly in her grasp.

"I'll be done in a moment, thank you." Her words came out sharp, and she didn't turn. She knew he'd have a scowl on what might otherwise be a handsome face. She wanted to write that in the last three days, the assistant keeper had brought with him storms of his own, but she didn't. She simply signed her name, set down the pen, and stood. "The ledger's all yours, Leo."

He shook his head, what appeared to be sorrow flashing in his dark eyes. "Please don't call me that. My name is Leonard."

Libby took a step back, bumping into the chair she'd just exited. She waved her hands against the silliness of his offense, holding back a grin. "I meant no harm, *Leonard*. Excuse me."

She fled the room but stopped in the doorway. The assistant keeper set her teeth on edge. Not only was he mysterious, as Owen had rightly assessed, but he was a bubbling brew of bitterness. He never smiled, and a small gap between his two front teeth allowed him an irritating, low-pitched whistle, which he did often, and did now, to her dismay.

She studied him as he sat in *her* place at the desk. The man was infuriating!

Who was this stranger? He wore handmade trousers, a

calico muslin shirt, well-worn suspenders, and a pair of old boots, so he didn't come from wealth. Though his fleeting glances at her refused to give up his hidden past, the longer he lived under their roof, the more curious she became as to what that past consisted of. Surely, the boatload of secrets tucked under that wiry hair of his begged to be uncovered.

She headed to the solace of the back porch, but as she passed the large black iron poodle doorstop that had been a treasure of her mama's, she stubbed her toe on it. "Ouch!"

Did she break her pinky toe, even with her boots on? It felt that way.

She hobbled to the wicker chair and plunked down, unlaced her boot, gingerly removed it and her sock, and rubbed her throbbing little toe. She'd had altercations with that poodle before, but this was the worst. She groaned as she massaged it.

"Are you all right? I heard you scream." Leonard spoke through the screen door. For the first time, he didn't sound mad. He sounded concerned.

"I'm fine, and I didn't scream. I stubbed my toe." Libby wasn't about to give him any reason to care for her.

"A delicate little woman such as yourself should be careful. You could break something."

Now she was angry!

She stood, whipped around, and thrust her hands on her hips. She narrowed her eyes and fairly growled. "Excuse me. I am not a delicate little woman. I can hold my own against the best of them, especially you. And I'd appreciate it if you'd leave me in peace—in *my* home."

She stood there, boring a hole through the screen until Leonard retreated. He never apologized. Never said he was sorry. What a discourteous, ill-mannered man! She rubbed her foot a few more minutes and carefully slipped it into her boot.

"Need help lacing that up, my wee chickadee?" Owen rounded the corner and peeked through the railing like a little boy. His baby blues reflected the sunshine, and his grin held a bit of mischief. How charming he could be!

"I'm fine, but thanks." Libby straightened the tongue of her shoe.

He stepped toward her but stopped at the steps. "Want me to help with the milking? I've already mucked out the stalls, swept the walkways, and cleaned up the debris that was blown in by the storm. I can't be shirkin,' so I'm at your service, my lovely lass."

She studied him and grinned. Not ten minutes after she accused Owen of being jealous, he'd begged forgiveness for walking away. Moreover, he was such a servant. Always ready to help, like now. Owen wasn't all prickles and stings like Leonard.

She laced her boot, tying it tight. "That would be grand, sir. Later this afternoon, we'll all be heading to the Independence Day festivities, so I'd like to get all the chores done while it's still cool. Alberta is fixing a wonderful picnic to take into the village."

She waved for him to take the empty chair next to her, so he stepped onto the porch and joined her. "Aye, I forgot. Today is the Fourth of July. America's Independence Day, is it not? Canada has a similar holiday, but it's July first and called the 'Anniversary of Confederation.' I'm sad we missed it."

Libby viewed Wolfe Island across the channel. "Yes, I've heard. Are you from Canada, do you suppose?"

Owen raked his hands through his hair and frowned. "I wish I knew, Libby. I'm weary of not knowing."

She placed a hand on his forearm. "Maybe there's a reason you can't remember. Or you don't want to remember. Maybe something bad happened, or a sad past keeps you from recalling it."

"Perhaps. I'm praying for a breakthrough. Soon."

She prayed he'd remember everything soon, but she also worried about it, fearing everything might change. As they sat together in comfortable silence for a few moments, she breathed in the tangy smell of the mighty St. Lawrence and the sweet scent of the nearby honeysuckle. The warm, briny lake breeze tussled her curls and tickled her neck, while the rhythm of the gentle waves calmed her concerns. For now.

She stood. "Shall I milk the cow while you brush down Chief. Then we can check the garden before it gets too hot?"

He reached for her hand but quickly withdrew his, shoving both into his pockets. "Aye, let's."

As they headed to the barn and garden beyond, conflicting emotions and questions flooded her mind. If he were Canadian, would she ever see him again when he left? How could she live without him—and with that hired help?

She stuffed her worries for the moment, and after she milked Bess, she searched for a few early-harvest vegetables for their picnic. Now and again, she peeked at Owen weeding and patting down varmint holes. His sun-kissed skin glistened with sweat, and his strong arms bulged under his linen shirt. Dirt smudged his face, and mud tainted the knees of his trousers. He'd make a mighty fine farmer.

When he removed his cap, sweat-moistened hair spiked up in all directions. He swiped his face with his forearm, sending the hairs of his eyebrows standing up in an almost comical way. She giggled as she joined him, showing him her basket of finds.

"I guess the three days of rain helped the garden grow. I found several carrots and beets and two handfuls of beans. It's amazing how one day, crops are not quite ready, but the next, they are. Alberta will be thrilled, and you'll be amazed at the magic she'll do with them."

"It's been three days, darlin'. A lot can happen in three days. And you do your own magic, Libby. I assure you."

What he alluded to, she wasn't sure. But she blossomed like a rose under his abundant affirmation. He was so quick to compliment her, so unlike her papa and certainly not her brother.

She caught a whiff of Owen's sandalwood scent—smooth, creamy, rich, and earthy. Her face grew warm as she stared at him. If only he could stay here forever.

He took her basket and motioned toward the house, Buoy galloping up to them. He reached down and petted the dog's head. "Hello, you scrappy old boy. And how are you today? Blathers! You're all wet. Have you been saving another soul?"

Libby laughed. "He loves the water, that's for sure. Light-keepers prefer large dogs who like water, and Papa has trained him well. He's a skilled and loyal dog who can be sent into the waves to rescue shipwrecked people when the keeper can't reach them. But you're the only one he's had the privilege of rescuing so far, and I'm glad of it."

Owen chuckled as they headed to the house. "Aye, and I'm grateful for him and for you. Shall we enjoy this beautiful morning on the porch with books and a glass of tea? That way, Buoy can dry in sunshine."

She dipped her chin, but sad thoughts made tears prick the back of her eyelids. Like weeds fighting in her garden, loneliness sprouted at the thought of Owen leaving soon.

~

The early evening sun shone brightly over the Cape Vincent village green as Owen reveled in the villagers celebrating around him. Cape Vincent seemed to be a tight-knit community of people who cared for each other. The young and old, the rich and poor, even the jabbering busybodies and gossips.

He could envision himself living here. With Libby.

Far better than in a big, impersonal, noisy city.

Dr. Renicks waved a hand, bidding him to visit. "Good evening, Owen. And how are you faring these days?"

"Fit as a fiddle, save my spotty memory, Doctor. I remember the strangest things at random times, but I still can't recall my surname or where I'm from. I have to admit, it's a rotten bit of luck, and I'm growing more frustrated with it by the day. Is there anything I can do?"

The tall, elderly gentleman removed his round spectacles and wiped them on a handkerchief he pulled from his pocket. "I'm afraid not, but be patient, young man. It might only take one little trigger to unscramble the mind. I've sent word hither and yon inquiring if a man such as yourself is missing from all over the north country, and so has the sheriff. So far, we've heard nothing."

Libby joined them with Connie by her side. "Happy Fourth, Dr. Renicks. How are you?"

Dr. Renicks acknowledged Connie with a slight nod. "I'm fine, thank you, Libby. I see your patient is still in process."

She tossed a gentle smile Owen's way. "Yes, but we'll keep hoping for answers."

The kind doctor laid a gentle hand on her shoulder. "I must be going, but keep me updated."

Once they bid Dr. Renicks a good evening, Connie curtsied ever so slightly. "Hello, Owen. I'm sorry I haven't been out to the lighthouse lately. I've been ever so busy with midwifery. Seems half the women in the county are birthing babies these days."

He nodded. "Good evening, Nurse Connie. I understand. Libby's been a great help."

Libby chuckled, the sound so sweet it tickled his insides and warmed his heart. "A precious new life comes first. Will you join us for the evening? Alberta made a mountain of food, and you simply must see how big Ralph is. He's walking now."

Owen liked the sound of *we* and *us*.

Connie shook her head. "I saw Ralph and Alberta a few

minutes ago, but I'm sorry to say that I already have plans with the Burgess family. I'll come and visit soon."

Libby and Connie hugged goodbye, and Owen bid the nurse farewell. They joined Alberta on the patchwork quilt laid out for their picnic, but wee Ralph wiggled in his mother's arms until she rolled her eyes. "How am I going to serve this food if you run off, little man?"

Libby scooted up on her haunches. "I can."

Alberta huffed. "Thanks, but I'd rather have a break from this squirming child. He's been a handful all day, and with his father working late again, I'm plumb wore out."

Libby scooped up her nephew. She set him on his feet and took both of his tiny hands in hers. "Let's go for a walk, shall we? Relax, Alberta. We'll return soon."

Owen hopped up. "May I join you? I'd like to stretch my legs on this crackin' evening."

Libby chuckled at his Irish saying, and Alberta grinned as Mr. Montonna returned from talking with a friend. "I'm glad Leonard took the watch tonight. I haven't seen Arnie for ages, and it does a body good to have a break."

Libby patted her father's arm. "I'm happy for you, Papa. You two go ahead and eat. I'm going to tire this little one out. We'll eat when we get back."

Mr. Montonna gave Owen a stern look as he took the child's left hand from her. He pretended not to notice the lightkeeper's objection and addressed Libby. "It'll be easier to walk with the wee lad between us."

A twinkle in her eye and a smile on her lips contrasted with her papa's steely gaze. Her father disapproved. He'd already told him so. But what was a man to do? She clearly needed help with the child.

They wove through the tapestry of blankets and picnickers, and a few people stopped them to say hello or comment on how big Ralph had gotten. But then, as they passed the woman who had gossiped about Libby at the hardware store, he over-heard her comment to her husband, "That's the rogue who has been seducing the lighthouse girl all summer. Scandalous!"

A few yards beyond them, Libby suddenly tripped over a tree root that had surfaced above the grass. She fell to her knees but caught herself on all fours. Thankfully, she had let go of Ralph, so the child wasn't hurt.

Owen lifted a rather stunned and embarrassed Libby by her waist, as if she were a slight girl, and set her upright. Her light-blue skirt had muddy marks along the front of it, and her cheeks were red as tomatoes, but otherwise, she appeared unharmed.

Libby pointed to the child. "Quick! Get Ralphie. He's toddling toward the road."

Blathers! In his haste to help Libby, he'd let go of the lad's hand. He sprinted to the toddler, scooped him in his arms, and returned to the tykes's aunt. "Whew! That lad can take off faster than a rabbit. I think I'll carry him."

He put him on his shoulders, and Ralph giggled, patting Owen's straw hat as if it were a drum. Ignoring those who stared, he turned to assess Libby again. "Are you all right?"

She brushed her skirt and took a step but faltered. "I think I twisted my ankle."

He gave her his arm, and she slipped her hand in the crook of it, while he held Ralph tight on his shoulders with the other. "Hold on to me. Let's get you back to your family."

When they returned to the picnic, Mr. Montonna's glare slipped to his arm, warning him he was crossing a line.

His heart thudded in his chest until he could hear only that, and he fought the reality that her father didn't approve of him. Probably never would.

Alberta stood and took her son. "What happened to you three? You weren't gone long. Libby, your dress. Are you all right?"

Libby told them their tale, and they ate dinner in silence, lost in their own thoughts. Owen squared his shoulders and kept his chin high under the scrutiny of the lightkeeper.

Dusk crept in like a sneaky schoolboy. Then twilight turned to night, and an owl hooted from the tree above his head. Crickets chirped their evening tune. Bullfrogs croaked back and forth. Stars popped out on the velvety canopy of the heavens. A full moon painted a road of gold on the river, and fireflies began their nightly dance, twinkling gaily until fireworks overshadowed them.

The boom and crackle of the initial exploding illuminations elicited a collective cheer throughout the crowd. Then a plethora of whirling, bursting, shooting fireworks lit up the sky with glimmering, sparkling beauty that almost hurt the eyes. The acrid, smoky smell of burning chemicals followed, but the experience stirred a flittering emotion that brought tears to his eyes.

The fireworks display was beautiful but short lived. Such as he'd seen in the city.

What city? Where did he belong? He searched his memory for an answer.

Libby tugged her shawl tighter around her shoulders and leaned in close to him. "Wasn't that magical?"

He glanced at her angelic face, a battle raging within him like an anchor weighing him down. He scooted away from her as casually as he could, but her brows furrowed at his action, her eyes questioning him. Irritation prickled his scalp and ran down his back between his shoulder blades. He pinched the bridge of his nose to fight back fears that threatened to reveal the grief within him.

In the eyes of her family, as long as he didn't know who he was, he'd never be good enough for her.

He was a stranger. An outsider.

A nobody.

CHAPTER 10

The next day, Libby peeled potatoes while Alberta prepared the chicken to roast. "Lieutenant Worthington is inspecting the light at the moment. After lunch, I expect he'll finish inspecting the grounds, including the house. I'm glad it isn't laundry day, or the place would be a mess. We'll have to watch little Ralph, though, and keep the house tidy."

Alberta slipped the chicken in the oven and wiped her hands on a towel. "Yes, we want Papa to get his award again this year, so I thank you for helping with my boy. He's a busy one, that's for sure. Last night, Will told me the lighthouse inspector is the son of a former inspector who once worked in this area. It's interesting how sons so often follow in their father's footsteps. I wonder if little Ralph will follow in Will's footsteps and become a lightkeeper too."

Libby took the towel and hung it on its hook. "I wonder what Owen's father does."

Alberta flashed warning with her dark eyes and chewed her bottom lip as she always did when she was upset. "Be careful,

Libby. Your father and brother don't want you involved with that stranger."

Libby rolled out the dough for biscuits and sighed. "I don't understand. Papa is lost in his grief, but he doesn't want me to be happy. Will is mad at me. Leonard is simply unbearable. And Owen is hot and then cold, engaged and then aloof, all in a mere moment. What is wrong with all of them?"

"Men can be confusing, but I have to agree with your papa and Will as far as Owen goes. Who knows what's going on with Leonard. And Owen? Perhaps he's beginning to realize that he doesn't belong here and is pulling away to protect you."

Libby wanted to scream. She needed air before she said something mean. She wiped her hands on her apron and removed it. Alberta had always been gentle, kind, compassionate. But now she was siding with Papa and Will?

"I'm going to tell Papa about dinner. Be back soon."

She hurried out the door before her sister-in-law could say anything more. Why were they all against her? Owen might not know his last name, but he'd proven his worth and displayed his stalwart character time and time again.

Libby climbed the tower to join her father and Lieutenant Worthington. She found them out on the parapet discussing several points of the inspection and assessed them from the lantern room.

Papa, as always, was handsomely attired in his lightkeeper's uniform, the ornaments on his sleeves and the golden embroidery on his lapels sparkling in the sunlight. Leonard was also there, dressed in the unadorned blue uniform that assistant keepers wore.

Lieutenant Worthington's uniform was pressed and tailored impeccably. He was tall, thin, and elegantly official. And though he had a small, thin mustache, the dapper man's youth surprised her. Why, he couldn't be much older than herself. How did he get such a distinctive position at so young an age?

She stepped into the fresh air but stood back and listened instead of interrupting them.

The inspector read his assessment that he'd recorded in his ledger. "The glass prisms in the Fresnel lens are pristine. So is the bronze pedestal. Even the copper oil pitcher is sparkling, and the weights and gears that rotate the lens look brand new. The mechanisms work flawlessly, and the floor is spotless. Not a single spider or fly within the entire lighthouse. Everything is in tip-top order up here. Well done!"

Papa grinned. "We use feather dusters so we don't scratch the lens and spirits of wine to clean off the dirt, grease, and oil. A bit of rouge polishes the brass and lens."

Leonard spoke up, his voice tainted with conceit. "I clean the windows every morning and evening. Not a smear or smudge. And we trim the wick and refill the oil every three hours without fail."

Lieutenant Worthington furrowed his brow at the assistant keeper's arrogant tone. "How long have you been here, sir?"

Leonard withered. "Almost a week."

Papa grinned, pointing to the light. "This beam can be seen up to twenty miles. The Wolfe Island folks often comment on it."

Libby stepped forward. "Excuse me, please, but dinner will be ready within the hour." She waved her hand toward the sparkling St. Lawrence. "Isn't this a beautiful view?"

Lieutenant Worthington clicked his tongue. "It is. Catching a glimpse of the area from the lighthouse towers up and down the St. Lawrence and Lake Ontario is one of the perks of my job. Besides, I get to meet fine folks like you. Last week, I inspected Rock Island Lighthouse and met the new wife of the keeper. But enough chatter. We should be finished with the lower levels of the tower inspection within the hour. Thank you, miss."

Libby acknowledged his comments but took an extra

minute to admire the midday beauty. This tip of land where the lake joined the narrow river granted her a unique view that few enjoyed. Like a necklace of shimmering gems, the body of Lake Ontario met the St. Lawrence River under the high-noon sunshine, sparkling like jewels. It brought peace that little else could. It was exactly what she needed to calm her frustrations concerning Alberta.

The men continued to talk as she excused herself, descended the ladder, and paused at the first landing, leaning against the wall for a moment. She read one of her favorite quotes aloud. "'Books are lighthouses erected in the great sea of time—E.P. Whipple.'"

She chuckled at remembering the teasing she'd gotten when she wrote it. Will had called her his baby sister bookworm, but the light inspector at the time wrote it down for his daughter's benefit, saying that she, too, loved books.

She descended the last flight of stairs and stopped. She'd best find Owen and tell him about dinner, too, since he'd made himself scarce after breakfast. Was it due to the inspector or her?

Libby stepped out of the tower into the bright sunshine that blinded her for a moment. The soothing smell of baked chicken urged her to hurry to Owen and then return to help Alberta. As she neared the horse corral, the pungent odor accosted her nose, and she wrinkled it against the stench. She found Owen mucking out the mess, faithful as the day was long.

"Dinner is within the hour. I hope you're hungry. Alberta and I have been making a feast for the inspector."

Owen stopped and stared at her. "I wonder if I should stay away, since I'm not part of the family. I don't want to put a black mark on the inspection."

Libby moved closer to him and placed her hand on the wooden fence between them. "A lightkeeper's calling is to aid a sailor in need. It's part of his job, so you're more than welcome."

"But have I not outlived my welcome? It's been almost two months. What would the inspector say about that?"

Libby stepped onto the bottom board of the fence. "I believe he'd say, 'Well done, Mr. Montonna. You've cared for this man, and he's been a great help around the lighthouse property.'"

Owen nodded. "I thank you for that. I'll come. If you're sure."

Libby hopped down. "I'm sure. See you soon."

Before he could object further, Libby ran to the house to help Alberta with a much better attitude than when she'd left. She'd barely entered the kitchen before her sister-in-law wiped her forehead with her forearm and said, "Please get Ralphie. He's been crying for several minutes, but I didn't want to leave the dinner to burn. He may need his diaper changed. I wish he would have slept through dinner."

Libby was partway up the stairs before she responded. "On my way. Coming, nephew!"

When she reached his room, little Ralph was standing in his crib, rocking the railing and wailing at the top of his lungs. Will had made a fine bed for the child, with the sides high enough to keep him safe. But as the boy rattled it, she feared he'd soon be strong enough to tip the whole thing over.

"Settle down, little man. Do you need a change?"

She tugged him out of the crib, and sure enough, he needed a full change, diaper and clothing too. Thankfully, Alberta had a pitcher and basin at the ready, and before long, Ralphie was clean, dressed, and ready for inspection.

He chewed on a wooden darning egg she'd given him, drooling as he cooed happily. But as she hiked him on her hip to descend the steep steps, he tried wiggling free.

"Let me carry you down the steps, child. Then you can walk or crawl or run to Mommy if you want to."

She kissed him on the temple and held him tight, and he finally settled down. But what would they do with this rambunctious lad during a dinner with the lighthouse inspector?

⁓

*O*wen entered the cottage hesitantly, still unsure if he'd be welcome. He'd regret it if the inspector thought him a breach of the lightkeeper's duties.

Mr. Montonna beckoned him to the table with an amiable attitude quite different than the night before. "Come and join us, son."

He complied, taking the only empty seat, nearest Libby. "Thank you, sir. I'm sorry I'm late. The billy goat escaped again, and I had to chase him halfway to the neighbor's farm."

Libby giggled into her napkin.

Mr. Montonna guffawed, then he pointed at Owen and turned to the inspector. "This is the man I was telling you about who washed up on our shore in May. He has whitewashed the oil shed, tower, cottage, outhouse, and barn. He's cared for the animals like a seasoned farmer, and he's also been helping Libby with the garden. All for a few vittles and a place to lay his head. I daresay, he deserves a great deal of credit for making the property look so good, and I will miss him when he leaves."

Owen smiled, but before he could thank Mr. Montonna, the inspector reached out his hand. "Lieutenant James Worthington. Pleased to meet you. On behalf of the New York State Lighthouse Board, we are grateful for all you've done. Now, tell me a little about yourself, if you please. Perhaps I can be of service to you."

Owen sucked in a deep breath, grateful he wasn't being shunned or viewed as a problem. After they blessed the food, filled their plates, and began to eat, he told the lieutenant what wee bit he remembered of his shipwreck and his past life.

"But what I do know, Lieutenant Worthington, is what a splendid lightkeeper and family you have serving here. They have cared for me tirelessly, sacrificed their time and privacy, and been the best representation of what it is to care for your neighbor that a man could ever experience. There's an Irish blessing I want to extend to this family, 'May neighbors respect you, trouble neglect you, the angels protect you, and heaven accept you.'"

Leonard groaned loudly, glowering at Owen. In return, the lieutenant, Mr. Montonna, and Libby all scowled back at the assistant keeper.

Owen ignored the man. "Pardon if I ask, but where are Alberta and wee Ralph? Are they all right?"

Libby swallowed her food before answering. "They went for a walk, and she took a picnic lunch to share with him. You know how active the boy is."

"Shall I go and relieve her? I could watch the tyke so Alberta can be here with you."

Mr. Montonna shook his head. "Always willing to help, this one. Alberta has been in the kitchen all morning making this fine meal, and I expect she's happy to be in the sunshine with her son."

Thankfully, Libby veered the conversation back to the inspector as she rose and refilled the coffee cups. "Tell us about yourself, please, lieutenant."

The inspector patted his lips with his napkin. "Since graduation, I've been stationed in Buffalo with my father who inspects the lighthouses along the western shores of Lake Ontario. But the inspector for this region recently suffered a heart attack, so I've been assigned the St. Lawrence to cover for him this summer. Actually, in 1885, my father inspected the lighthouses here. The same year you took this position, correct, Mr. Montonna?"

Libby's father glanced at the ceiling. "Yes, and I remember him! He spoke of his son, but I never connected the dots. My son, Will, hopes to follow in my footsteps too."

Lieutenant Worthington's face brightened. "We'll have to put in a good word for him. I must admit, I'm pleased to be here. I joined my father that summer of '85, and I fell in love with the Thousand Islands. Just this week, I inspected Sister's Island Lighthouse, where I was reacquainted with a childhood playmate who is now training to replace his father one day. My father and I stayed at the Thousand Island House in Alexandria Bay that summer. Do you know it?"

Mr. Montonna smiled. "I took my wife to the balls there several times. She adored getting all dressed up and dancing to the Steubgen Orchestra."

The inspector nodded, grinning. "I adored my teacher, Miss Addison Bell. Had a terrible crush on her for years. But the highlight of that summer was meeting President Chester Arthur. He was fishing in the islands, and I mistakenly hid in his boat. He didn't find me until we were out near Wellesley Island, and he helped me catch my very first fish, a feisty sturgeon. But I nearly got a whipping for scaring my father and half of the town. Thankfully, the president calmed Papa down, and all was well."

"What a delightful adventure." Libby stood. "On that happy ending, would anyone like a piece of huckleberry pie warm from the oven?"

The lieutenant and Mr. Montonna murmured, "Yes, please," almost in unison and followed it with laughter. But Leonard cast a shadow over their mirth. Why was he so troubled? He'd moped the entire meal, and his sullenness made it obvious that he wasn't pleased with anything.

Lieutenant Worthington broke into Owen's musings. "Back

to business, if you don't mind. The kerosene you are using, sir, is far too volatile, so for safety, let's get you a new iron oil house that'll hold 540 gallons or so. And I'll petition Congress to finally approve a permanent assistant keeper position and a cottage for him to be built next summer. How's that?"

Just then, Alberta returned with Ralph. She greeted the inspector but promptly excused herself to take the baby upstairs for a much-needed nap.

Mr. Montonna grinned wide, his dark eyes shining delight. "I'd be much obliged. With our growing family, we're running out of room in here. After the pie, would you like to see the rest of the house and property?"

Libby set liberal slices of warm pie in front of each of them and filled their coffee cups.

When Lieutenant Worthington took a bite, he moaned. "This tastes like my grandmother's. What a treat! Thank you for a fine meal. And yes, we'd best make our way through the outbuildings so I can catch the boat back to Clayton. After I finish my pie."

Libby tittered. "We don't always eat this well, but the rains have yielded abundant wild berries, and our garden is growing nicely."

Lieutenant Worthington swallowed the last of his pie before speaking. "You are blessed. Not every lighthouse has such vast resources and land."

By the end of the day, Lieutenant Worthington had inspected every inch of the cottage, barn, garden, oil house, cistern, and even the corral and outhouse. After he'd left, they all breathed a sigh of relief as Owen joined them for a supper of cold leftovers.

After the meal, Owen relaxed on the porch, but the summertime humidity brought sweat to his brow. He wiped it with his handkerchief. What a day! Had the inspector given good marks? He hoped so.

Once the dishes were done, Libby joined him. He set down the newspaper he was reading and stood to greet her. "Ready to enjoy a quiet ending to a busy day?"

She inclined her head but said nothing. She simply stood at the edge of the stairs and stared at the setting sun, seemingly lost in the beauty of the summer's eve, though her brows furrowed with concern.

The stress of the inspector had set his nerves on edge, and he guessed, hers too. "Lighthouses silently shine their beacon of hope against the bleakest night." He gazed at the tower as his strained words came out stilted and weak. "I wish the good Lord would shine a light into my memory. The darkness is shrouding me in hopelessness."

Libby reached to pat his arm, but she lost her balance and would have fallen down the stairs had he not caught her in his arms. Her lithe form, warm under his hands, sparked feelings he couldn't name. But all his senses stood at attention.

The smell of lilac in her hair. The softness of her skin. The warmth in her eyes. The faint scent of homemade soap. Had he never been near a woman?

He set her aright and cupped her chin with his hands. Gently. Tenderly. Longingly.

She pressed into it, lowering her gaze. He felt a tiny quiver, but when she raised her eyes to his, they revealed delight, not fear. Then her lips trembled and opened, as if she were going to speak. But instead, she wet them with her tongue.

Owen had to stop this. "We mustn't. Your family wouldn't approve."

She blinked as if in agreement, but the lass's gaze spoke of sadness, uncertainty, lostness...the same as he felt.

"They're not my family. I was adopted." The ache in her voice almost made him cry.

"What do you mean?"

Libby took him by the hand and led him to the shore. Then

she told him the entire, tragic story, including the deep sorrow of not belonging, of being betrayed. How could her mother do that? "Please don't say anything. Mama swore me to secrecy, but I had to tell someone."

Owen wrapped her in his arms, caring less if her father or Will or even Alberta saw and sent him packing. Libby trusted him.

As twilight fell around them, Libby sobbed, much like the Irish keeners at a wake, until she could cry no more. When she'd spent all her tears, she sighed, swallowed her sadness, and said but two words. "Thank you."

Like a thorny rosebush, random memories pricked Owen's mind, but none of that mattered now. How could he leave this woman who trusted him? Needed him?

He couldn't.

He wouldn't.

Ever.

CHAPTER 11

*J*t was barely daybreak, but Libby couldn't wait to see Owen. Last night, Papa had shown her the bucket he'd found during the inspection. The flotsam she'd found the day after Owen came to her shore. She itched to see if the cap and sailcloth were his, but he'd already retired for the night.

Libby ran to the barn, daring to hope she held keys to unlock the man's memories. When Owen saw her, he stopped brushing down the horse and waved, so she joined him, still panting from her exertion and excitement. She took a moment to catch her breath before speaking.

"Good morning, Owen. I have a surprise for you. Yesterday, Papa found these in the cellar when they were inspecting it. I'd tucked them away while you were recovering and forgotten all about them. Any chance they could be yours?"

She handed Owen the captain's cap as well as the piece of sailcloth she'd found on the shore. He needed answers to renew his hope, and she'd love to be the one to give him that gift.

Owen examined the navy-blue cap, damaged by water and mildewed to ruin. His eyes grew wide, and he ran shaking fingers over the patch on the front that sported a crest in the shape of a shield. On the shield was a crown, two open books, and what looked like a beaver.

He blinked several times and groaned. His reply was barely above a whisper. "*Velut arbor aevo* means, 'As a tree through the ages.' It's the University of Toronto's motto. Where I got my engineering degree."

Libby gasped, placing her hand on her pounding chest. "You remember?"

"Aye." Owen blew out a ragged breath, his voice shaky. "I remember."

She squealed like a little girl who'd gotten a new pony on Christmas morning. "Tell me more. Tell me everything. Please? Oh, isn't it marvelous?"

He sighed, handing her the cap. He didn't even smile. Didn't rejoice. Didn't thank her for unlocking his prison door. Instead, he looked as though he'd seen a ghost.

He inspected the damaged sailcloth in his hands, rubbing it nervously. He turned white as a winter's snow, and tiny beads of sweat popped out on his brow even though it was still the cool of the morning. His eyes teared, and he spoke with a quivering frown.

"I had ignored the storm's warnings and kept the sail trimmed way too long. But then, when I saw I was nearing a dangerous, rocky shoal, I frantically lowered it. At that moment, the crashing waves tipped the boat, and the boom must have broken free and struck me. I remember being pummeled by the frigid St. Lawrence. But that's all I remember, until I saw your lovely face hover over me that day. How did I survive that and make it to your shore? By the grace of God, I suppose."

Libby touched his arm. He trembled, tears forming at the corners of his eyes. His lips quivered.

His sadness confused her. Why wasn't he overjoyed to finally remember? He'd hoped for it for so long.

His gaze pleaded with her to exonerate him. "I remember more, but I fear you won't like it."

Libby clicked her tongue. "Remember what I shared with you about who I am—and who I'm not? We all have things in our past we want to keep locked in a closet, hidden from others because they embarrass or pain us. But if it's the truth, please share it. I want to know all about you. Your past can't be worse than mine."

Owen swiped his hand through his hair. "It is, I'm sorry to say, for what you want me to share was birthed of my own folly."

He hesitated, but she encouraged him on. "I've come to know that you are a fine man with a good heart. Nothing from your past could taint that. But no secrets. You must always be truthful with me, and though it may not be who you are now, I want to know who you were."

He shrugged, raised his brows, and pressed his lips together, as if to apologize, the anguish turning his eyes icy. "I'd been an excellent swimmer in both boarding school and university, winning awards as well as the affections of pretty women. I'm ashamed to say it, but I'd broken more than one heart and confused many. Aye, I'd been a cad, Libby. That I remember, and I'm not proud of it."

Libby cringed at his confession. What was he trying to tell her? Did he have a lover somewhere? A wife and children, perhaps?

He handed her the sailcloth and put out his palm like a stop sign. "Wait here, please. I'll tell you all I remember in a moment. I promise. Then you can flee from this rake if you want to."

Thank goodness, she had a moment to gather her wits after his stunning confession. But what more might he reveal? Who was this man she'd come to love? To trust? Was it all a ghastly mishap set on destroying the last bits of hope she had to love and be loved? And if her papa and brother knew about his past, they'd surely forbid her to even talk to him, let alone marry him.

He returned with the pocket watch little Abe had found. He opened it and placed it in her hand, then pointed to the engraving, *To MDS. From Father.*

"A tiny piece of memory dogged me every time I looked at this thing. But until now, I couldn't recollect why. It was my grandfather's watch. His name was Martin David Shanahan. *MDS*. I am Martin Owen Shanahan, the second. After my father who gave this watch to me."

She handed the pocket watch back to him. "This is a fine and costly piece. And the University of Toronto? Truly, you're a man of wealth and status, as I thought."

"Aye. I suppose so."

The admission gave her no solace, and by the melancholy tone of his words and the doleful expression on his face, it didn't comfort him either. "But why did you remember only your middle name and not Martin, your first name?"

"I don't know. I only remember this watch and what I've told you. It also brings to mind my kind grandfather who died when I was but a lad. Yet I still can't remember where I live or even what my father looks like, but I suspect I'm from Canada as you suggested."

Libby swallowed, gathering her nerve to ask the next, and more important, question. "Are you married? Do you have a family?"

Owen stiffened, as if he'd been accosted by an icy wind. His eyes narrowed and brows furrowed, so suspicion slithered through Libby's veins, slowing the flow of blood like a December winter. Did she hit the mark?

"I...I don't think so, but I can't say for certain. I'm so sorry, Libby, but all of that is still a muddled mess. How can I remember one thing but not everything? It exasperates and bedevils me. How can I dream of a life here, with you, in the midst of all this befuddlement? What future could you have with a man like me?"

What future, indeed? Her family would disown her. Wait... they weren't really her family, were they? Those upstanding, Bible-toting, church-going, moral people she'd loved all her life had lied to her. About who she really was!

Disown her? Why shouldn't she disown them?

Something deep inside her broke. Until now, she'd been heartsore over her mama's confession—and her death. She'd been imprisoned by Mama's mandate to keep the truth of who she was a secret. And for a while, she'd been so hurt and felt so betrayed that she had tried to deny her mama ever divulged that she wasn't her own child. But she did. And now?

Now, she was angry. Angry at the lies. Angry at being forced to keep a secret. Angry at her mama—and her father. And angry at having to be afraid to love a man who was kind and good and...truthful!

She'd had enough.

Libby slipped her hand into the crook of Owen's arm. "The shadows of yesteryear won't help you find the wind in your sails to move forward. Perhaps we shouldn't go mucking around in the past. If things come to you, fine. We'll deal with them. But don't force them. They'll only bring pain. Your past is past. Let's move forward."

Owen shook his head as though he was coming out of a deep sleep. Bewilderment masked his comely face. "What?"

She had to make him understand. She'd take him as he was, a sordid past or no past at all. Papa didn't need to know. Neither did Will or Alberta or anyone else. She could run away with Owen, and they could create a new family.

She could keep her own secrets too.

"Don't drag yesterday's woes into today's joys. And when

you're free, don't look back. We can make our own future free from the past."

Owen took her hands in his and pressed a tender kiss to her knuckles. "Truth is, I love you, Libby. But until I know everything, I can't face the future with or without you."

A mixture of joy and apprehension filled her thoughts, bringing tears to her eyes. She wanted to tell him she loved him, too, but she couldn't risk rejection. What if he never found out everything about his past?

Without him, how could she face the future either?

❧

Two days later, when Tom Bennett, the livery man, pulled up in his best carriage, Owen waved. The man had often given people rides to see the lighthouse, but it was well past visiting hours. Who wanted to come here at this hour?

Owen walked toward them and greeted Tom while his passenger, a middle-aged gentleman in fine attire, stepped out of the carriage. Owen acknowledged the balding visitor backlit by the setting sun. Something about the man niggled at the recesses of his mind as he came into the light.

Owen put out his hand. "Welcome to Tibbetts Point Lighthouse. How can I help, sir?"

The man frowned, glaring at Owen until he adjusted his collar. What was wrong? After a narrowed-eyed scowl, the man shook his head. "Really, son?"

Owen pulled back his hand and plunged both into his pockets. "Sir? How can I help?"

The man clicked his tongue. "All right. I'll play along. I'm Martin Shanahan, father of Martin Owen Shanahan, the second, of Toronto, Canada. I own a thriving boat-building business and have come to fetch my son home to take it over one day—and to not miss his wedding."

Owen groaned, as if punched in the stomach. His head spun, and a cold fear crawled up his spine. How did he know his name? Could all he said be true?

"What?"

Something about the man, and what he pronounced, rang a distant bell, so tiny that Owen could barely hear it tinkle. He swallowed his apprehension. "That's *my* name, but I don't remember you *or* the details of which you speak."

Mr. Shanahan's face turned red as the nearby roses. Was the man having angina? Mr. Shanahan's voice shook with anger. "Stop it, son! I have no time for games."

"I'm not playing games."

Mr. Shanahan's mouth dropped open, and the man withered before his eyes. His shoulders slumped. His brows drooped. His face paled. "You...you really don't know who I am? I am your father. You disappeared in our yacht over two months ago, and we thought you dead. But a Lt. Worthington passed your description around the harbor, so I came to see if it was you."

Like a thick fog bank lifting off the lake, the confusion in Owen's head began to clear. Slowly at first. Then faster and faster, like the movie he'd seen at last year's 1893 Chicago World's Fair.

A strict, opinionated, prejudiced father who was forcing him to marry his partner's daughter, Chelsey, though she was fat, ugly, and void of personality. A mother who died a year after his big brother, when he was only ten. A lonely existence at boarding school.

A cottage near the Canadian town of Kingston. Sneaking away to captain the yacht. A sudden storm. Waves and thunder and lightning—and darkness.

Buoy. Libby. Tibbetts Point Lighthouse. Then finding the peace and joy and love he craved.

And more.

Owen's heart beat so fast and strong, he feared the man could hear it. His palms sweated and so did his brow. "Father."

He recoiled at the revelation, his tone flatter than he'd planned. The past weeks had brought him more love than he'd known in a decade.

Forever, maybe.

Father clapped him on the shoulder, then settled his hand on his rather large paunch. "Glad to see that you remember me. I've had the authorities searching for you high and low all across Ontario. I didn't dream you were hiding in another country. In this tiny New York village, no less. I'm only glad that Worthington fellow came to Toronto, or you might have missed your own wedding. It's in two weeks, you know, and Chelsey is beside herself with worry."

Owen swallowed his horror, and his heart took to beating triple time, causing sweat to wet his forehead even more. He swiped it with his shirtsleeve. "There will be no wedding, Father. I was going to call it off when I returned from my outing on the river, but, well... I won't be pawned off on her or anyone else I don't love."

Father guffawed, reminding Owen of all the times the man had ridiculed, mocked, and demeaned him from the time he was but a wee lad. "What's love got to do with it? We're building an empire, son. With your marriage, our business will be secure."

Owen's head began to throb, so he rubbed his temples with the heels of his hands. He couldn't think. Couldn't deal with this. "I'm sorry, Father. I'm feeling rather poorly. Can we continue this conversation another time, please?"

Father assessed the descending sun and acquiesced. "Very

well. I'm staying at the Roxy Hotel. Come for breakfast, eight o'clock sharp, and we'll discuss plans for your return."

It was impossible to say *no* to Father. His head hurt. His memories jumbled. His heart ached. "Tomorrow, then. Good-night, Father."

Owen moaned as his father got into the carriage, a heaviness filling his heart, his mind, and the very breath he breathed.

He needed to talk to Libby, but she'd been feeling poorly and had sequestered herself to her room all day. He couldn't intrude on the ailing lass. Her father and brother would skin him alive.

He raised his eyes to the cloudy sky. "What now, Lord?"

~

*A*fter a sleepless, fret-filled night, Owen recalled the rest of his past—the many details of his life both good and bad. Though Owen longed to talk to Libby before he had breakfast with his father, she hadn't yet appeared from her sickbed, and he couldn't force entrance. So he saddled Chief and headed into town.

Along with the flood of memories came a mixture of pain, anger, frustration, regret, and helplessness. His father had always been overbearing, demanding, and uncaring. But he'd not win this round. Owen had to overcome.

Somehow.

When Owen joined his father at the Roxy Hotel's best table, he pasted on a smile. "Good morning, Father."

His father took a puff of his cigar and continued reading the paper without acknowledging him for several moments. Then he slowly folded his paper and set it on the table. He removed his spectacles and huffed. "You're late."

Father never had anything positive to say to him. Never. Not when he got top grades at school. Not when he graduated from college with honors. Not when he did everything his father asked him to do.

No wonder his mind had refused to remember the pain of the past.

Owen ran his hand through his hair. "Actually, I was here early, but the maître d' was busy seating other parties."

Father harrumphed as the waiter brought plates for both of them and poured coffee. "I already ordered for us."

Once the waiter left, Father took a gulp of his coffee, bit off a piece of bacon, and began. "As I said yesterday, you need to return to Toronto immediately. The wedding plans are in motion, and I've kept your office and position waiting for you, but my patience has expired. We'll take the ferry to Wolfe Island and then to Kingston and transport from there. It's all been arranged. We leave at eleven."

Of course, Father had already made plans, like a little god sitting on his throne commanding—no, demanding—complete obedience.

"I'm sorry, Father, but that is impossible. I will not marry Chelsey, and I can't return to the business. As I've tried to tell you time and again, and recalled vividly during my sleepless night, I want to be a journalist. Always have. Always will. The boat-building business is *your* passion. Not mine."

Father turned scarlet again. "See here, *boy*." He kept his voice low, but vehemence and vitriol tainted his words. "Your grandfather came to Canada during the Potato Famine and built the business from nothing. I built it up more. You will too. And you *will* marry Chelsey, or you can kiss your rather substantial inheritance goodbye."

Owen's indignation tightened his jaw and prickled his scalp. He took a sip of his coffee. *Steady on. Be firm but respectful.*

"So be it. Truth is, I've found the woman I want to marry. She's a good woman who loves me and fills my heart with joy."

"Well, I'll be. You, a betrothed man, taking up with a rustic, rural American from this nothing village. It's ridiculous."

"First, I didn't know I was betrothed. I'd been injured in the shipwreck and only two days ago discovered my identity and elements of my past. Second, I never agreed to this match, and I don't love Chelsey. Third, Libby is a godly, kind woman who will make me happy and support me in my work."

Father snickered. "Happy? Marriage is for building wealth, not for finding happiness. You, son, have all your priorities wrong. What would your dead mother and brother think of you betraying our family to marry an American and forsaking our business?"

"Mother would say, 'God be with you,' and Stephen wouldn't care, God bless their souls. I am a man and must follow my heart, Father, even if it means disobeying you."

"This is more than disobedience. This is dereliction of duty. It is rebellion. It is family treason!"

Blathers! Father could be so dramatic.

After taking a bite of toast, Owen willed his voice steady. "Nevertheless, my place is here. With Libby. And, one day, I hope to run a newspaper as I've always dreamed."

"Your mother was a fool to cater to your journalistic tendencies, even as a boy. A newspaperman's salary? That'll barely put food on the table. How will you support this girl?"

Could Father be softening?

"I'll work hard, Father. Her family are lighthouse keepers who have helped me heal. *She* helped me heal."

"Lighthouse keepers? What kind of life is that? They work grueling hours for little pay while putting their lives in danger. Fools. All of them. Mark my words. You'll not get a penny from me if you abandon your heritage, *and* you'll be the laughingstock of all the well-to-dos in Toronto. In all of Canada, perhaps. Don't be a fool, son."

Could he risk giving up a promising career and financial security to pursue a career and a dream that might not provide for Libby and him?

CHAPTER 12

*L*ibby swiped the hair off her face, thankful her headache had passed with a day in bed and a long night's sleep. As she dried the last dish, the scent of a coming storm tickled her nose and warned her at the same time. The day would be a blustery one at best.

But where was Owen? He hadn't come to breakfast, and Papa said he'd taken Chief and gone into the village. At such an early hour and on a stormy day like this one? But why?

Lightning split the darkening sky with a crackle and a pop, followed by thunder that shook the house and rattled the windows. She hurried into the parlor, pulled back the curtains, and peeked out the glass to admire nature's spectacle.

Clouds scudded across the sky, then collided as they formed a steely thunderhead, pushed by the impending storm. Within minutes, the heavens turned an eerie gray, and bright lightning lit the sky followed by a distant rumble and a sudden loud thunderclap. A deluge drenched Tibbetts Point in an instant.

What if Owen was stuck in town all day? Or worse, if he was

caught in the downpour and lightning storm returning from town?

As Libby stared out the window, footsteps echoed on the front porch, so she quickly opened the door to find Owen soaked clear through and white as the winter snow. She took his hand and pulled him inside. "Are you all right? I was just now warming a kettle for tea—and worrying about you."

Owen scrubbed his face with a hand and swallowed hard. "We need to talk." His words came out clipped and shaky. "Someplace private."

She assessed the seriousness of his words. Though Papa was sleeping, and Alberta was upstairs feeding Ralphie, the house wasn't always private. And Leonard, likely brooding in his room feet from them, could appear at any moment. No. The cottage wouldn't do.

"Why don't you change and meet me in the tower? No one's there this morning. Take Papa's slicker. I'll use this one."

She handed him the slicker, and he slipped out the door and into the storm. She had to learn what vexed him so, and regardless of what it was, she would face a thousand storms to be with him.

Yesterday's sick day in her room had given her time to think. Time to assess her situation away from all distractions. Could she really stay with a family who'd only pretended to be her own and lied to her? And what of the gossip spreading around town? Even Connie had warned her about the tattling toadies. All summer, the church services and trips into the village had become dreaded events, for glares and whispers abounded. Perhaps she should strike out on her own, find work in Watertown or another city, and be done with it.

Or maybe Owen was her providential rescuer. But more than that. Just as he admitted he loved her, she realized that she loved him back. Perhaps...

Libby hurried to the kitchen and moved the kettle to the

back of the stove. She donned the oversized slicker, floppy rain-hat, and her mud boots, and she ran through the downpour to the lighthouse. Though it was a mere twenty or so feet from their back door, by the time she got to the tower, her face and hands were as wet as if she'd taken a dip in the river.

She removed her soaked things, swiped her face and hands with her shirtsleeve, and climbed the steps to the light. Though summer thunderstorms could be terrifying at the top, they were also magnificent. Owen had yet to see a good gully washer from up there. Its resplendence might even settle him down.

But what on earth was the matter with him? She'd never seen him so flustered, not even when he discovered the less respectable parts of his past. Had he recalled something more sinister or malevolent?

She clambered into the lantern room and surveyed the storm. Nothing but rivulets of rain, whistling wind, and flashes of lightning all around her. The storm quickly began its crescendo, rumbling with a deep bass of thunder followed by the incessant sound of rain thumping on the windows.

At the echo of footfalls in the tower, she bent down and hollered into the hatch door from whence she'd come. "Owen? Is that you?"

"Aye. Coming!" His voice sad but urgent.

Within minutes, he joined her, his alluring face now drawn as if he hadn't slept a wink. Worse still, his eyes held a deep anguish that frightened her. He swallowed, heaving to catch his breath.

She placed a gentle hand on his forearm. "Tell me what's tormenting you. Please."

With tangible sadness tainted by acrimony, Owen chronicled everything, his voice quivering all the while. Several times, he turned his back to her, swiping at tears, no doubt.

He recounted his father's surprise visit to Tibbetts Point the night before. The unwelcome revelation of who his father was

—and who Owen was. He also told her about Chelsey and the impending wedding and the dreadful order that he return to Toronto and assume his place in the family boat business. And he related his father's demands—and his threats. When he was finished, he blew out a breath and moaned.

Libby moaned too. What was to become of their hope for a future together she'd dreamed about last night? The love he'd confessed only a few days ago—and that she felt for him? The hope for tomorrow?

"What will you do, Owen? Or is it 'Martin'?"

"It's Owen. My mother always called me that with such love and sense of belonging that Owen I shall always be. I remembered that last night. And I remembered my true passion."

Libby gasped. Did he love this Chelsey, his intended? "Your passion?"

Owen squared his shoulders, and his tone transformed from anguish to zeal. "Aye. I've always wanted to be a journalist, ever since I was a wee thing. Mother encouraged me to make a family newspaper, and I'd write all kinds of silly articles. About the spider web in our cellar or our dog having puppies. Mother died when I was ten, and all that ended. Papa spoke only of the boating business and forbid me to talk of the written word."

Libby glanced at the tempestuous day outside before turning to Owen. "I'm so sorry for your loss."

He shrugged, running a finger along the edge of the lamp as if he were admiring it. "My neighbor ran the weekly newspaper, and I often visited him at his office. He'd let me watch the type-setter take pieces of fonts and arrange them into composites, which were used to make the printing plates. Mr. Hollingsworth said it was a difficult skill to learn because you had to read backward. But when I read an entire plate backward with ease, he said that I was a mighty smart lad, and he'd bet a dollar to a dime that I could be a successful journalist. Then he let me write a few articles, and he printed them in our newspaper though I was only eleven. They were mostly simple stories about firemen saving a cat or Santa coming to town, but I was hooked. And although I got my engineering degree, I took several journalism classes at university too. That, Libby, is what I want to do with my life. Spread the written word. Provide readers with stories that inform and inspire. Not sit in an office and help Father make money."

Lightning illuminated the room, as if to punctuate Owen's admission. But the boom of the thunder came several seconds later, and it was much quieter. The storm was retreating. Hopefully, Owen's storm would too.

He paused as if formulating his next words, so she waited, lovingly patting his forearm.

"Father wants to meet you, but perhaps we should pay it no heed. I'm not so sure it's a good idea for you to encounter such a stern man. He was going to leave today, but with this storm, he'll stay until the morning, hoping I'll return with him."

From what he'd said about his father, he sounded formidable. Maybe even ruthless. But he was Owen's father, and she had to win him over. "The storm is subsiding. I'd like to meet him."

Owen scooped her in his arms and hugged her tightly. He planted a kiss on the top of her head, heaving a sigh so deep his chest rose and fell under her cheek. She listened to his heartbeat racing a mile a minute, until it settled to a strong and steady rhythm that comforted her. She held him tight, too, as if she never wanted to let him go.

In truth, she didn't.

"What's going on up here? This is highly inappropriate, Miss Montonna."

Leonard? How did she not hear him ascend?

In an instant, Libby and Owen dropped their arms and stepped away from each other. Now her heart raced at breakneck speed. What if Leonard told her papa?

"I...I was upset, is all. Owen was ... Excuse me, but this is none of your concern."

The assistant keeper's eyes narrowed, and a sideways smirk revealed volumes. "Even though it's still morning, with this storm, your papa thought it best to light the lamp, miss. I didn't expect to find...*this*."

Owen stepped into the fray. "You've found nothing amiss, sir. Now, if you'll excuse me, Libby, I have things to attend to."

Libby stood there dumbfounded as Owen slipped down the ladder, leaving her alone with Leonard. What could she say to the man who could destroy any hope of a future with the man she loved?

~

*R*eluctantly, Owen ushered Libby into his father's hotel suite and found him alone. No one to buffer his vehemence.

Blathers!

Father sat like a king on his throne, dressed in his finely tailored suit, casually smoking his fat cigar. When he met his father's stern and taunting gaze, the air crackled with tension.

Poor Libby. Too much like wee David before the frightful Goliath.

Perhaps he should have spared her the perilous challenge. How could she stand strong against this formidable foe? Could he?

"Father, may I introduce to you Elizabeth Eliza Montonna, daughter of Tibbett's Point Lighthouse keeper."

It wasn't a question. It was a statement.

For a moment, Libby's smile wavered, but then, she raised her chin, stood an inch taller, and pasted on a brilliance that buoyed his resolve to be her armor bearer through the battle.

His father's surly smirk was more to acknowledge than to

welcome. What sharp blade would the man lunge at Libby? His father had pierced his thin armor dozens of times, leaving wounds and scars that still ruled his life. Could he allow Father to attack her too?

Owen offered Libby his arm, and she took it, but when he faltered, she tugged him forward. He placed his hand securely over hers as it rested on his arm.

"So pleased to meet you, Mr. Shanahan. After all Owen has been through, I'm glad you found your son unscathed." Her most respectful and sincere tone baffled him. She clearly didn't discern his father's trickery.

Father harrumphed, but then turned on his treacherous, clandestine charm Owen had seen so many times before when the man attempted to win over a client or customer or foe. Owen's stomach flipped. Father was intent on subjugating Libby before attacking her.

Owen shifted his weight, glancing at the settee. He motioned toward it. "May we..."

"As I've told you since you were a toddler, 'speak only when spoken to, *boy*.'"

Father didn't offer them a seat, so they stood before him while he puffed his cigar, surveying Libby from head to toe with silent disdain. "So, little lady, what brings you here today?" With a clash of steel in his tone, the parry began.

Libby curtsied. "I've come to meet you, sir. Your son is a wonderful man and..."

Father guffawed. "...and you want to claim him."

To Owen's wonderment, Libby stood strong, like a seasoned queen meeting a kingly foe. So unlike her wilting demeanor around her family. Where did she find such bailiwick?

Her courage loosened Owen's tongue. "No, Father, she isn't *claiming* me. *I* intend to marry *her*."

Libby glanced at Owen, surprise and questions evident in her expression. He hadn't meant to say that.

Suddenly, his father's steely glare turned menacing.

"Tell me, *miss*...why would you want to ruin Owen's life by imprisoning him here in poverty and scandal? You would require him to forsake all he knows including country and family? What kind of love is that? You, little vixen, are nothing but a money-grubbing fraud."

Libby gasped, her free hand flying up to cover her heart. "Sir, I..."

Owen's pulse took to trotting, and the hair on the back of his neck stood up. "Now just a minute..."

Father pointed a fat finger at him. "Silence, *boy!*" He trained his narrowed glare on Libby. "Furthermore, *girl*, I've made inquiries about you. You're a foundling, an untoward orphan, and if you truly loved my son, you'd bid him farewell."

Father's words pierced Owen with sharp arrows meant for Libby. The deep wound of parental manipulation, control, and rejection hit its mark. The harsh reality of a hatred so deep took his breath away and rendered him silent.

Libby, however, was valorous in battle. "Sir, a lighthouse stands strong against the fiercest gale, the darkest night, the deadliest storm. Lighthouses don't move. They stand, unwavering in the storm and shine for all to see. A lighthouse can't stop the storm. It can't rescue the stranded. It can't save the day. It simply shines, guides, and brings hope. I pray, sir, that hope for the future and for a better relationship with your son will shine in your darkened heart one day."

Jab!

Father's eyes widened in disbelief as the truth sliced through his thick armor. Color drained from his face, and time seemed to cease. As if the chair beneath him shifted, he squirmed in his seat, grasping the arms until his knuckles whitened. The illusion of his authority crumbled before Owen's eyes.

His father was a cowardly lion.

But then, like a beast ready to pounce, Father sprang from his throne and thrust an arm toward them. He roared so loud, his valet burst through the door. Father ignored the interruption and took a step toward them. "Be gone! The both of you. I never want to see your faces again."

Owen led Libby toward the open door but stopped before exiting it. He turned and glowered at his father. "I agree with Libby. I pray you'll find hope and peace for your hard and darkened heart."

With that, they fled the hotel and stood in the street breathing in the fresh summer air. For several moments, neither said a word.

What a nitwit! How foolish he'd been to bring her here. "I'm so sorry about that, Libby. I should never have subjected you to such cruelty."

Libby shook her head. "But you didn't. Clearly, your father is a troubled soul."

Owen took Libby's hand and kissed her palm. "You were so brave in there, Libby. You fought like a skilled swordsman. I've watched politicians, millionaires, and other powerful men fall in battle to my father. But you, Queen Elizabeth, outshone them all. I, on the other hand..."

"Queen Elizabeth? Really, Owen." Libby *tsk*ed, patting his arm. "You, on the other hand, did the best you could against a man who wields his power unfairly, and I'll not fault you for that."

"But he used that power against you, and I will fault him for that!"

Libby shrugged. "I must confess, I surprised myself. Your father reminded me of a bully who taunted and teased me in school. Calvin pulled my braids and poured ink all over my test paper. He tripped me at recess, stole my lunch, and chased me halfway home more than once. I had nightmares about him for months, and he made my life miserable until I stood up to him and made him cry in front of the whole school. After that, he became my ally, and I pray your father will do the same one day."

Owen shrugged, hopelessness engulfing him. That wouldn't happen anytime soon. "That would take a miracle, and I'm afraid I haven't the faith for such."

Will pulled up next to them in their wagon, Buoy sitting tall beside him with his tongue hanging out. "Need a ride home?"

Libby nodded, reaching for his hand to help her into the seat. "Thanks, Will. I must admit, this has been a long, blustery day."

Owen climbed in on the other side of the wagon and sat next to her as she rubbed both of Buoy's ears while he lay at her feet. "Thanks, Will. What are you doing in town?"

Will leaned over his sister and glared at him. "I had errands to run, but I'd like to ask you the same."

Apparently, the storms weren't over.

Would they ever be?

CHAPTER 13

*L*ibby shook the dismay from her mind but blanched at her brother's acrimony. She rubbed her dog's head. "What is the matter with you, Will?"

Will shouted "giddy-up" a little too loudly, setting the horse and wagon in motion before answering her. "I saw you coming out of the Roxy. What in heaven's name were you two doing alone, in a hotel? No wonder the tattling toadies are in an uproar. I was in the hardware store just now, and Mrs. Pritchard gave me an earful. Why, the whole village is talking about you. I've had enough of it."

The implications of his suspicions hung in the air like the heavy summer humidity following the morning thunderstorm. She wiped her brow, her stomach constricting into a tight ball. She gulped a deep breath, swallowing the bile that rose with his filthy allegation. She had never dreamed an innocent meeting could be twisted into such vile claim—from family, no less.

But he wasn't her family, was he?

The tension from the meeting with Owen's father suddenly took its toll, and so did many of the innuendos the man had so ungenerously spewed. She withered under Will's unspoken accusation of inappropriate behavior.

Buoy licked her hand as he'd always done when she was sad. She tugged him closer to her legs for comfort.

Ever since Owen had come to Tibbetts Point, Will's distrust of her tainted their once-close relationship, their family, her world. Now he was accusing her of indiscretions that questioned the very foundation of her character?

Before she could push past the shock and formulate an appropriate retort, Owen came to her rescue. "Sir, I assure you, everything that transpired here was entirely above board. I brought Libby to the Roxy to introduce her to my father who is visiting from Toronto. Nothing inappropriate or untoward transpired, and Libby has consistently exhibited impeccable conduct. She is an upstanding, honest, virtuous woman with unblemished character. I believe you are well-acquainted with her virtues and should vouch for her without hesitation."

Will scoffed before glaring at Owen and shaking his head at Libby. "That's not what I've been told."

Libby shifted in her seat to glower at her brother. "And you believe the local gossips? How terribly disappointing."

"Not them. One who has seen your actions firsthand."

Libby let out a frustrated shriek, her exasperation surpassing the level she'd felt in the presence of Owen's father. She leaned forward, demanding an answer. "Who? Who do you believe over your own sister?"

He stared at her, and a flicker in his eyes questioned her very existence. "*Are* you my sister?"

The words hung in the air like sleet on a cold winter's day. He knew? But how? She looked at Owen, assessing whether he had broken his promise to keep her secret safe. He was the only person she'd ever told. Thankfully, Owen shook his head and gave an innocent shrug.

"What...what do you mean by that? What gave you the idea that I'm not your sister?"

Will stretched as if he were a stiff old man. "Rumors. Whispers. I'm tired of them, Libby. They're affecting our family. Alberta doesn't want to come into town anymore."

The sadness in Will's voice prompted tears to slither down her cheeks. Libby had held them back all day. But now, they wouldn't be held back. "I'm sorry."

Silence filled the rest of the ride back to the lighthouse. As soon as Will stopped the wagon, she pushed past Owen and scurried to the ground with Buoy following close behind. She picked up her skirts and ran into the house and up to her room, determined to be alone. To figure out what to do next.

But she couldn't think. All she could do was cry.

Within minutes, a knock interrupted her weeping. The door creaked open, and Alberta peeked in. "May I enter?"

Libby shook her head. "Please leave me alone. I need time to think. And don't bother calling me for dinner. I'm not hungry."

Alberta took two steps toward her before retreating. "All right. But there's trouble brewing downstairs, and Papa has called a family meeting for tonight, at seven sharp. Be ready with answers, dear."

Her sister-in-law closed the door, leaving her to ponder the implications of an inquisition. Papa hadn't called a family meeting since Mama died.

Was this one about Libby?

She must have fallen asleep, for she awoke to an incessant rap on her door. She shook herself awake and sat up. "Who is it?"

"Alberta. It's time for the meeting."

Libby glanced out her window to see the sun low in the sky. "Goodness! I fell asleep. I'll be down in a minute."

She straightened her hair and clothing and pinched her

pale cheeks. Was she heading to her doom? She still didn't know what to say, what to reveal, what to do.

She tossed up a quick prayer for wisdom.

When she entered the parlor, not only were Papa, Will, and Alberta there, but also Owen—and Leonard. The shock of their presence seized her like an explosion, shaking the very core of her. She stared at Owen, whose eyes were tainted with trepidation, and then at Leonard, who stared at the floor.

"I thought this was a *family* meeting."

Papa leaned toward her. "Have a seat, Libby. Our meeting includes necessary parties."

Libby sat in the empty chair near her papa, and her hands began to shake with the gravity of the moment. "Necessary? What's this about?"

Buoy joined the meeting and lay down by her feet. A furry comfort she needed then.

In the quietness of the parlor, her heart beat even louder than the tick of the clock on the mantel. The hushed tension grew as five pairs of eyes trained on her. Papa's gaze held a mixture of apprehension and resolve. Will's, a boatload of disappointment and confusion. Alberta's, watery with tears, suggested support and concern. And Owen's spoke of love. Compassionate love.

But why was Leonard here? Unlike the others who met her gaze, he stared at his feet, picking at his fingernails.

The group seemed to hold its collective breath as Papa squirmed in his seat, the chair creaking underneath him. He reached over and took her hand, the weight of the world etching deep lines on his aging face. "My darling Libby. There's something I need to tell you." His voice stained with regret and love. "A secret we've kept hidden for far too long."

Did everyone know her secret? Time seemed to stop, suspending her in a deep sense of dread. Confusion stirred her blood, making her dizzy, nauseous.

Papa wet his cracked lips. "When you were a little baby, your mama and I were blessed with a most precious gift. We adopted you into our family. Our love for you has never faltered, never wavered. I'm sorry it's taken me so long to tell you. I only wish your mama were here too."

He knew all along?

Buoy stretched and looked at her, his sad doggy eyes seeming to be filled with compassion. He leaned against her legs but then put his head between his paws.

An involuntary shiver ran through her as the overwhelming reality of the moment rattled her mind and body. She turned to Will and then to Alberta. "Did you two know?"

Will shrugged and beckoned Alberta to answer. "Not until a few days ago. I'd gone to the general store and overheard two women talking about you. Something about 'to think she's been putting on airs all these years, when she's nothing but an *orphan*.'"

A whimper escaped Libby's lips. "They said that about me?"

"They're pea brains, Libby." Alberta huffed. "And I'd heard enough malicious chatter to last a lifetime. You know I have a long fuse, but if you light it, watch out."

Will ducked his chin, a slight grin crossing his face before he swiped it away.

Alberta rolled her eyes. "Anyway, I strutted up to them and let them have it. 'How dare you?' I said. 'My sister-in-law is a blameless, honorable young woman. And you call yourself Christians? May the Lord judge your words.'"

Libby and Owen gasped in unison. Leonard sat still as a stone.

Libby swallowed her disbelief. "Thank you for supporting me, but you'll have the dickens to pay for that."

Alberta waved her concerns away. "You think I care? When I told Papa and Will about it, Papa explained the truth. But none of that matters, Libby. You are our sister, our family."

Papa reached over and hugged her, assuring her that her adoption only strengthened the love they had for her. "We love you, daughter."

Owen cleared his throat. "Tell them, Libby. It's time."

Should she? Yes! She was tired of keeping secrets. She heaved a steadying breath.

"Mama told me. On her deathbed. But she made me promise to keep it a secret. I almost told you, Alberta, but I didn't want to hurt any of you if you didn't know. So I told Owen."

Leonard began whistling, almost as a whisper. She turned to him, rising irritation prickling her. "And, pray tell, what are *you* doing here?"

He stood, stepping toward the door, never looking at her. "Excuse me, but it's time to light the lamp." He fled the house, and through the window, Libby watched him sprint to the tower and disappear.

Libby turned to her father. "Papa, please. What was Leonard doing here, and why did he leave?"

"He does have a part to play in all this, darlin', but I guess he wasn't ready to share the details. Please be patient. Everything will come to light in time. But even if it doesn't, nothing changes our love for you. Not even your mother's secrecy or mine. She only wanted to protect you. So did I."

Overwhelmed by their love, empathy, and honesty, tears began to fall. She swiped them away, determined to shed them in privacy. "Thanks, but right now, I need some time by myself."

With that, she climbed the stairs to grieve in her room.

Alone.

∾

*O*wen skirted around a large puddle, bumping his head on a low-hanging branch of a mature maple on his way to the shore. He rubbed the crown of his head, certain he'd have a goose egg before long.

What a turbulent ending to a terrible day!

He shuffled down the riverbank and found a rock to sit on as the sun slipped below the horizon, surrendering to the encroaching darkness with somber, muted hues of purple and burnt orange. Heaviness hovered in the air as a maelstrom of emotions churned inside him like the waters around a menacing shoal, ready to break him apart.

The day's trauma, compounded by the past two months, pummeled him into a turbulent, dangerous current, each memory tossing him in waves of disappointment, frustration, and pain. Like the morning's storm, thunderclaps of regret and lightning bolts of indignation bombarded his brain.

A sudden chilling breeze brought no comfort. Instead, it taunted him, mocked his cowardice. Twilight faded to deep darkness, and the mighty ships passing through the narrow river channel became haunting silhouettes. The mournful cadence of the river's waves hammered his conscience as an owl hooted scorn from the old oak above him.

His father's hateful accusations cut and sliced through his thoughts, leaving open wounds of resentment and anger. Each word a dagger. Each thrust of the sword jabbing at his past, his present, his future. His ruthless father had never concerned himself about what his son thought or wanted or cared about, and it had tainted his entire life.

But how dare he say such things to Libby?

His shoulders slumped as he recalled every heinous words his father spewed. Somehow, Libby had stayed unwavering under the sting of his venom, while he had withered like a delicate flower under the scorching sun. He had done too little to defend her. The thought of it turned his stomach.

As the cloudy night enveloped him, so did the darkness of his failure. He should have protected her from the monster he knew his father to be. How could he have let it happen? The bitterness of his inadequacy pressed upon him, suffocating him, gnawing at the fragile hope he had for a future with her.

How could he rectify his transgression? Maybe he should see his father and tell him what he thought, once and for all. No. Father would most certainly stand his ground, like a seasoned sea captain, and go down with his despicable ship if he had to.

Still, Owen had to do something, if only to assuage his guilt and failure and liberate Libby from his father's contempt. First thing in the morning, he'd go and defend her before the ferry took his father back to Canada.

That settled, he contemplated the depth of Libby's woes, so much more complicated and confusing than his own. The echo of Will's cutting comments likely left Libby with a wound that wouldn't soon heal. And on the heels of Father's and Will's ugly words, the poor lass had endured the confirmation of her adoption. How much more could she suffer before she shattered like fine crystal as it was smashed on the rocks?

He glanced up at Libby's bedroom window, now dark. If only he could talk with her now. Comfort her.

He groaned, rubbing his palm along the hard stone underneath him. His heart ached for the confusion, sorrow, and grief she faced. The horrifying shadows of this dreadful day must have shaken the foundation of her once-peaceful world, like the thunder had shaken the house that very day.

He bowed his head and prayed that Libby wouldn't be shipwrecked on the sea of uncertainty and heartache. That her grief wouldn't drown her. That the stormy days would soon pass.

But how could *he* help her? He'd have to wait until the morning.

"There you are, Owen." Will scrambled down the riverbank to join him. "I've been looking everywhere for you. Can we talk?"

Libby's brother settled on a rock next to him. When their eyes met, Will's gaze held a reticence that revealed his desire to have a difficult conversation. The cool breeze ceased, as if the very air around them held its breath, waiting for Will to carefully choose his words before he spoke.

"Owen, we believe it's time for you to be on your way. Our family, especially Libby, needs the time and space to heal. Though we've been patient while you recovered, my sister needs the same. Your presence only adds layers of complication to this troublesome season."

Owen swallowed hard. A mixture of sadness and surprise unsettled his thoughts. How could he support her if he wasn't here? Was leaving really the best way?

Will's tone held empathy, though he spoke firmly. "I know you care for Libby, and perhaps she cares for you too. But there are circumstances in which we need to give a person we care for the freedom to discover their own path to healing. Your presence would only impede that journey."

Silence fell between them, and hopelessness closed in on him. He couldn't go back to Canada, and he was no longer welcome here. Where would he go? And how could he leave Libby in such turmoil?

As if Will read his mind, he continued. "You're not abandoning her, Owen. Her family will take good care of her as the wounds mend and she discovers who she is without the added distractions you bring. I'm sure it's hard, but it's for the best." Will stood and patted Owen's shoulder before heading back to the house.

He sat there for a long while grappling with the mandate,

watching the light sweep over the river in a rhythmic motion. He glanced up at the tower to see Leonard out on the parapet looking down at him. Had he heard their conversation? With the stillness of the night, it was a distinct possibility.

But who was this churlish man who slithered in and out of their business? What secrets did he hold? Everything in Owen wanted to ascend that circular staircase and find out—with words or fists, he didn't care. But then where would he be? Vanquished? Shunned? Forbidden to ever see Libby again? He couldn't let that happen.

Instead, he climbed up the riverbank and sat on the porch. Sleep wouldn't come with his mind whirling. He would go, but how would he tell Libby he was leaving?

"Owen? Is that you?" Libby stepped onto the porch and sat beside him. "I have so much to tell you."

He needed to speak now, or he mightn't have the nerve later on. Or ever. "May I please speak first?"

Libby dipped her chin and smiled sweetly, but a long silence lingered between them, interrupted only by the cry of Ralphie in the room upstairs. When she smiled, affection sparked between them, but he ignored it as he rallied the courage to share his heart.

"Libby, it's time for me to be on my way." His voice cracked and faltered, and the sadness in it couldn't be denied.

Her brows furrowed in confusion as her eyes brimmed with tears. He was inflicting more pain on her, and his heart constricted at the thought of it. But he pressed on.

"I cannot stand to see you hurting—and worse, to be the source of your pain. You need to find your own way, free of my influence and distracting presence. You deserve to be at peace with your family and yourself."

An anguished tension settled between them until Libby blurted out a question. "Will you return to Toronto with your father and marry Chelsey?"

The incredulity of the statement forced a bitter cackle to escape his lips. "Lord, have mercy. Never! On either count. I'll find work somewhere, hopefully nearby."

Libby blew out a ragged breath and placed her hand on his. "Thank heavens. You scared me for a moment."

"I'm sorry you had to endure that just now. I'm sorrier, still, that I didn't defend you better to my father, Libby. Truth is, Father knows how to keep me in my place and render me a coward."

He slipped his hand from underneath hers, but she grabbed it with both of her hands and wouldn't let go. "You're not a coward. He didn't hurt me. I simply pictured myself with a huge shield around me, and I let the man's words bounce right off."

Owen's jaw dropped open. He snapped it shut. "Really?"

When the light made its rounds and illuminated the porch, Libby's eyes twinkled with pride. "Really. I wanted to meet him. After all, he's your father, but it obviously wasn't the best time to do that. Perhaps we'll meet under better circumstances one day."

He squeezed her hands, drawing the top one to his lips to kiss it. "Aye. I am not saying goodbye forever, Libby, but right now, me leaving is best for both of us. You need to figure things out, and so do I."

She kissed his hand back. "Perhaps, but how shall I endure?"

Indeed! Perhaps if he found a job and dispelled the ghosts of his past, he'd be able to give Libby everything she deserved... and so much more.

CHAPTER 14

$\mathcal{A}$s Libby stepped into her room and laid eyes on the surprise perched on her bed, a tiny gasp slipped from her lips. A bundle of letters neatly tied with a soft pink ribbon? The air hummed with quiet mystery, and she held her breath as she reached for them. Who had left them there?

A sense of anticipation caused her heart to race as she carefully untied the ribbon and ran her trembling fingers over the lovely feminine script. A tinge of trepidation pricked at her as she flipped through the bundle.

Each letter was carefully adorned with her full given name, Elizabeth Eliza Montonna, and a number from one to twenty-one. The envelopes, yellowed by time, held promises of stories and revelations and secrets that both scared and thrilled her. Would they bring joy, sorrow, or both?

She began with the first one, cautiously slipping her finger under the sealed pouch, slipping the single sheet of paper from it, and unfolding it carefully. The date on it was December 4, 1874. The day of her birth.

Her eyes scanned the formal handwriting to the bottom of the page. The signature? *Your mother.*

It wasn't Mama's handwriting. Could it be? A whimper caught in her throat. "Gracious, Lord in heaven! How?"

She held the paper to her chest as tears trickled down her cheeks. Could this day be more pregnant with emotion, with revelation, with surprise?

She swiped her tears until they no longer blurred the words that spoke of devotion. Love from her birth mother. Love that transcended time and distance. She savored each word, reveling in the testament of her mother's abiding desire for her daughter she had entrusted to the Montonnas.

The letter also revealed the sordid story her papa hadn't revealed.

Her mother wrote that when a sailor harbored in the village and had his way with her, she was but seventeen. Libby's grandmother had already passed, and her grandfather was a stern man, sending his daughter away in disgrace.

But her mother wanted her baby girl to know the love of a fine Christian family, and Mama had been her birth mother's friend. So, though she entrusted Libby to the lightkeepers, it was the hardest thing she'd ever done.

That first letter revealed love and sacrifice that dispelled the shameful shadows of her conception and adoption and settled her heart. The writer ended the letter with, *You will always be in my heart, my precious daughter, and my love for you will surpass space and time until I meet you in heaven.*

She didn't plan to meet her before? But why?

Was she alive? Where? Questions bombarded her brain until she shook free of them. She had twenty more letters to read!

She opened the next, and the next, each carefully dated, the last one only a month ago. With each successive missive, Libby learned chapters of her story unknown to her and pondered the revelations. That her mother's maiden name was Lucy Row, and she grew up in Brockville, Canada. That, a year after Libby was born, her mother married a wonderful man and soon had a child. In the most recent letter, Libby learned that her aunt, her mother's sister, Emma, had married the Rock Island Lighthouse keeper last month. That her cousin, her mother's niece, Julia, was visiting Sister's Island for the summer. So much to ponder. So many threads of connection.

The heartbeats of a mother's love seemed to pulse from the page, strong and secure. Her tiny room, a retreat for weeping just hours ago, now became a chapel for rejoicing. A sacred space of revelation and healing.

As she read the chronicles of a young mother who carried her for nine months and reluctantly gave her to another as an unselfish act of love, Libby began to understand the facets of who she was then, who she was now, and who she might become.

Unfettered hope began to spring anew.

She picked up the pink ribbon and rubbed it between her fingers—a connecting thread spanning two decades and who knew how much distance. Would she ever get to meet her birth mother? And how did the letters come to her?

She had to know!

She kissed the ribbon, caressing it for a moment against her cheek as she'd seen Alberta do with baby Ralph. She gently set the ribbon and the letters on her dresser and gave them a little pat before exiting her room.

She'd start with Papa. The light under his door confirmed he wasn't asleep, so she knocked gently and slowly opened the door.

Papa sat in his chair, Bible in his lap, a winsome grin taking years off his face. He slipped off his spectacles and sighed. "You found them."

Libby ran to her papa and threw her arms around his neck, kissing his cheek, joy spilling over. "Thank you, Papa. They were wonderful. So much love and learning. But why did you wait so long to give them to me?"

Papa's weathered face lost its mirth, etching lines of remorse that brought with it a melancholy sadness. He gulped in a breath, and his eyes brimmed with tears. "I'm sorry for keeping the truth from you all this time. We worried about your acceptance in the community and feared the village gossips and teasing from the children would taint your childhood with rumors and innuendos. It wasn't from lack of love, my darling daughter. Fear ruled us."

Her father's confession, rife with regret, illuminated the reason for the long-held secret. Instead of anger, compassion took its rightful place.

Understanding dawned. "That's why Mama doted over me so. I thought it was because I was a girl."

Papa chuckled as he set his Bible on the side table along with his spectacles. "That too. She loved you as her own, Libby, and so do I. I have to admit that I worried the prattlers would demand to know who your mother and father were, and that would have been ruinous to your future. If others knew ..."

Libby placed her hand on his. "Mother told me in her letters. But now, no more secrets."

Two big tears trickled down Papa's leathery cheeks. "We thought we were protecting you by keeping it a secret. I see now that we were wrong, and for that, I'm so sorry. Forgive me?"

Libby wiped his tears with her shirtsleeve and planted another kiss on his cheek. "Of course, Papa."

His confession and her mother's letters dispelled the power that the secret had over her and released a healing blend of acceptance and compassion.

He pulled her onto his lap and hugged her as if she were a small child. She settled into his arms as he squeezed her tight.

"About the letters, Libby. I didn't have them. Someone else

felt it was high time for you to know, and I believe they were brought to you from a place of love."

Libby pulled back to look him in the eyes. "Who, Papa? I want to thank them for bringing me this precious gift."

Papa sucked in a deep breath, and his eyes flashed concern, but for several moments, they sat in silence while he measured his words before speaking. She'd seen it a hundred times and respected him for it. So she waited until his wisdom of years broke the silence.

"Not everyone is who they seem to be. Life has a way of surprising us, showing us the unexpected. We need to be open to the wonder of a godsend that comes in an unusual package."

What was he alluding to? Could Owen be the courier of such blessings? But how?

Papa patted her hand. "There are people that may enter our lives as bearers of hope and light, though they may not appear to be so. That gift might be a shared moment or a kind word. Or it might be a revelation that changes the way we see the world. Embrace those moments, Libby, for they can change your life."

Papa's wisdom flowed like a gentle river. His words lingered in the atmosphere, confusing her but also bringing hope.

Libby laid her head on his chest and listened to his heartbeat. "Mama once said, 'appearances can be deceiving.' Perhaps that applies here?"

Papa gurgled a chuckle, causing her cheek to bounce off his chest. "More than you know, my darling child." His words held mischief.

Now he was teasing her. Like old times. Her papa was coming back from the shadows too. Perhaps the courier was the author of the missives?

At the thought, Libby jumped off his lap and fairly danced a jig. "Who's the messenger, Papa? Is it my mother? Is she here? Oh, please say yes!"

His eyes widened with surprise, and he leaned forward, a

frown replacing the smile. "Sorry, no. But you'll find him in the tower."

Confusion slapped her across the face, sending her off balance. She rocked on her heels. "In the tower? But ..."

Papa waved his hand. "Go, child. Go and see."

Libby nodded and fled the room. She hurried down the steps and out onto the porch before taking a breath, where she found Owen, sitting in his usual spot, Buoy at his side.

"Owen. You're still up. Come with me. Now!"

She reached for his hand and tugged him from his chair, but he halted.

"What's the matter? Are you okay?"

Libby shuffled excitedly. "Yes. Come and see. I want you there." She bent down and gave Buoy a scratch. "Stay here, boy. We'll be back."

Owen wasn't the courier.

But who was?

~

Owen followed Libby up the tower steps, puzzled by her urgency that she failed to articulate. What on earth was going on? Why were they frantically ascending the lighthouse at this late hour?

They climbed into the lantern room and found Leonard out on the parapet. No wonder. The heat in the room had to be close to one hundred degrees.

"Come." Libby waved, bidding Owen to join her outside. She'd barely stepped through the door before addressing the young man who turned to meet them. "Leonard, Papa sent me. Do you have something to tell me?"

What was she talking about? Leonard, the strange and secretive assistant keeper? What import would he have on this overwhelming day?

Owen hung back near the door, observing the two in the light of the full moon. At Libby's insistence, he'd come to observe and didn't want to be involved unnecessarily, but he was ready to help her if needed. He'd protect Libby with his life.

Leonard stared at her for several moments before answering her plea. "I wondered when you'd come. But why is Owen here?"

The assistant keeper stared at him. He worked his jaw with a tension Owen couldn't help but notice. Then the air thickened, and gnats encircled them. They swatted at them, but the tiny insects kept coming, teasing them.

Leonard huffed. "Blasted gnats. Every night at this time."

Moonlight illuminated Libby's quivering lips. "Please, Leonard. I want him here with me. Tell me what you have to say."

Leonard shrugged, his face stoic. "I told your father already. That's why I was at your family meeting. But, in the emotion of it all, I didn't think it was the best time to share my news."

Libby frowned, a puzzled expression on her pretty face. "I don't understand."

Something about the mysterious Leonard had changed, as if a weight had been lifted from him. He seemed lighter. His eyes brighter. His face softer. His voice even held a tinge of compassion.

Owen grew anxious for Leonard to spill the beans and release whatever secret he carried. But the assistant keeper slowly stretched, reminiscent of a cat awakening from slumber, hinting at a release of tension. Then he interlocked his fingers behind his head and stretched again, perhaps to find momentary freedom from the shackles that bound him.

The man was an enigma, a shadowy fellow that sent a shiver up Owen's spine. He'd better not hurt her, or he'd be sorry he ever came here.

"I'm not who you think I am." As if to punctuate his statement, Leonard swatted at the gnats and swiped his forehead with his shirtsleeve.

Libby glanced back at Owen with a mixture of confusion and frustration, but she turned back to Leonard and held her tongue.

As if the veil of secrecy suddenly fell from him, Leonard wet his lips, stepped up to Libby, and took her hand.

She stiffened and took a tiny step backward, letting out a surprised gasp. "Sir?"

Should Owen intervene? Save her from another overwhelming confrontation? Could she bear anymore?

Leonard finally broke the silence. "Elizabeth Eliza Montonna..." His voice was shaky but determined. "It is I who brought those letters to you. Our mother wanted you to have them. I am your half brother."

As he spoke, the words seemed to catch in his throat, heavy with profound significance.

As if lightning had struck between them, Libby yanked back her hand and grabbed ahold of the railing. "Owen. Come here. Please."

Owen flew to her side to steady her by placing his hand on the small of her back. He slipped his handkerchief from his pocket and pressed it into her hand. He forced a kind smile toward Leonard, begging him without words to be gentle. He gave the man a nod to proceed.

Leonard understood. "Our mother wanted you to know of her love for you and the lifelong journey she's taken with you in her heart. She entrusted me to bridge the gap between you and her and assure you of that love."

Libby began to sob quietly, her face hidden in Owen's handkerchief. She leaned into him, so he wrapped her in a hug.

An almost imperceptible grin flashed across Leonard's face.

"Mother would be pleased to know you are loved, Libby. By him. By them."

Libby's eyes widened, and a mixture of surprise and revelation flickered in them. She slipped out of Owen's embrace and tentatively hugged Leonard. "You're truly my brother?"

Leonard stiffly hugged her back. "I am."

Behind her brother's stoic façade, Owen detected grief even deeper than family secrets. An untold sorrow, carefully concealed, oozed from the depths of his eyes and in the way he conducted himself. What intricate layers of pain and loss did he carry? Perhaps it was time for him to be free too?

Owen placed a gentle hand on his shoulder. "Thank you, Leonard, for sharing this. And I appreciate that you allowed me to witness this special moment. But I also believe Libby would like to know more about you. Besides, it's high time every secret be out in the open, yes?"

For several long moments, they stood there lost in the plethora of emotions each one surely held.

Finally, Leonard stepped away from his sister and stood at the railing as Libby had done. They joined him, the air thick with silence and suspense. Owen prayed for the man, for Libby, for the moment.

"I had a family once, but now it's just our ma—and you. A few months ago, in the merciless throes of childbirth, I lost my wife and son in one terrible moment. My pa passed two years ago, but our ma is well and lives in Ogdensburg. She'd like to keep on writing to you, and possibly meet one day, if you are amenable."

Libby nodded vigorously. "Of course, I am! But please, tell me more about yourself."

Leonard slowly, cautiously described his pain and anguish. In that vulnerable moment, he bared his soul, allowing two near-strangers to witness the weight of his shattered world. When he finished, his confession hung heavy in the air.

Libby hugged her brother again, this time more genuinely. "I'm so sorry for your loss, but I'm glad you came, brother."

Owen stepped to the other side of the assistant keeper. "I'm sorry for your loss too."

He didn't know what else to say, but he knew this moment, this day would leave an indelible mark on all their hearts. Silently, he bent his head and thanked the Lord that he was here to bear witness to the mystery of secrets uncovered and shattered hearts on the road to healing. If only his could begin to heal too.

Owen took a deep breath of the fresh night air. "Charles Dickens said, 'No one is useless in this world who lightens the burdens of another.' You've done a fine job of lightening Libby's burdens this day."

Libby touched her half brother's arm. "Remember, we are here now to help lighten yours."

Leonard studied each of them for a moment, but then he surveyed his surroundings. "Thank you. I'll keep that in mind. Now, if you'll excuse me, I have work to do."

The moment had passed, but it was a precious one. Owen and Libby bid Leonard a good evening and climbed down the ladder and steps and into the cool air where Buoy lay patiently waiting for them.

Owen gave the dog a head rub, then grabbed Libby's hand and tugged her toward him. "Before we end this tumultuous, terrible, wonderful, amazing day, I have things to say."

Libby's eyes danced with emotion. "I, sir, have no words left. So speak on."

Owen hadn't formulated his thoughts. How could he put them into words? He glanced at the starry sky before studying her face. "My darling Libby, the God who dropped me at your shore and allowed us to love each other knows the secret longings of our hearts. As certainly as He arranged the constellations in the night sky so sailors can safely navigate. And He placed you into a family who loves you and cares for you. He protected you and planted you in this amazing little corner of the world, and He's with you in all of it. Should the doubts and questions of the future and the fears and pain of the past overshadow the love He has for you? For me? For us?"

He paused and kissed her hand. "My heart belongs to you, Elizabeth Eliza Montonna, and I will return for you as soon as I can. In the meantime, I will write to you, and we must trust Him to order our life. He won't ever leave you or forget you or turn His eyes from you, and neither will I."

CHAPTER 15

*A*s the Thanksgiving sun rose high in the unusually warm, November sky, Libby and her family climbed into the wagon waiting just outside the barn. She no longer feared attending church or cringed at seeing the villagers. She no longer worried what any of them might say.

After last month's poignant sermon on the power of words, the chattering gossips had fallen silent. Indeed, several had surprisingly reached out to her with smiles and welcomes and words that allowed forgiveness to heal and bridge, bringing joy to life. Even Will had shown her extra attention—along with that loving brotherly teasing she'd always enjoyed. Indeed, the very atmosphere of Cape Vincent seemed to radiate transformative, heavenly kindness.

As Libby entered her childhood church, the commitment to that benevolence echoed with greetings and hugs and well wishes. Her heart warmed at the change. Though a few holdovers still stole questioning glimpses her way, none voiced their disapproval of her, and she no longer cared what those few might think. She was free.

She took a seat in the polished pew as the familiar scent of aging hymnals brought comfort. The bright morning sunlight streamed through stained-glass windows, casting rainbows and vibrant colors that seemed to rejoice with her.

On this special day of Thanksgiving, Libby recalled the journey of forgiveness she'd trod, how the shadows of sorrow had been replaced by hope and joy. She bowed her head to offer thanks for the healing she'd experienced.

She peeked at her papa, once a bearer of secrets. She thought of her mama, the secret sharer whom she'd forgiven and would see again in heaven one day. Her brother, sister-in-law, and nephew, a loving, supportive family. Such a tumultuous year, her odyssey from anger to resentment to melancholy to peace.

Hope and harmony with others had blossomed in her choice to forgive. Her thoughts meandered to her birth mother, the letters, her half brother, and the affection that came with them. Through them, forgiveness had built a bridge from the past to the present, and she trekked to and from it with gratitude.

The service began with the minister interrupting her musings. "Let us stand and sing, 'It is Well with my Soul.'"

Her mama's favorite hymn. How appropriate. Her mama had told her the tale of how it came to be written several times, and it made the song all the more poignant.

The author, Horatio Spafford, had lost his fortune in the 1871 Chicago fire, and soon after, his son had died of scarlet fever. Not two years later, his wife and four daughters were sailing to England when their ship sank, killing all four of their daughters. Only his wife survived. In response to all this tumult and tragedy, the man chose faith.

Libby sang out loud, her heart now full of faith.

> *When peace like a river, attendeth my way*
> *When sorrows like sea billows roll*

Whatever my lot, thou hast taught me to say
It is well, it is well, with my soul

She chose. Chose forgiveness, faith, and love. And it changed her.

The pastor stepped forward to share the thanksgiving words of wisdom, and Libby joined the congregation in hushed anticipation. She was indeed grateful—for her heart's healing and for hope for a bright future.

On the day following the pivotal "secret smashing," as she came to call it, Owen had embarked on his own journey. And every letter from him since created a solid foundation of trust and hope for a wonderful life together one day.

A week after Owen left, Leonard returned to Ogdensburg, his countenance lighter than when he'd come, having fulfilled his obligations, he said. Will negotiated with farmer Grayson to work both at Tibbetts and the farm for reduced pay. And Libby pitched in to help even more than before.

"Today, as we give thanks, let us reflect on the importance of voicing our gratitude. The simple act of blessing others with words of thanksgiving can change a person's life."

Libby wiggled in her seat, the creak of the wooden bench alerting others that she was daydreaming. She sat up straighter, focusing on the minister's words.

"Let us never forget to thank God—and others—for the simple joys of life and the people who share them with us. And remember to give thanks to God, even for the challenges, for they shape us, make us better people, and draw us nearer to Him. As we enjoy this holiday, and every day, be grateful. A grateful heart turns the ordinary into extraordinary, just as Jesus turned water into wine."

When the minister gave the final blessing and dismissed them, neighbors and friends immediately put his admonitions into practice—except for Alberta, who fled the church to change Ralphie's stinky diaper. Libby's papa affirmed Dr. Renicks. Will thanked Mr. Grayson for understanding about his need to work at the lighthouse.

Libby hurried over to Connie, who sat across the aisle from her. "Connie, thank you for being a faithful friend. My dearest friend. I'm so proud of you and all you've accomplished as a nurse, as a person. How you care for our community so sacrificially. How you're always ready to help others in need."

Connie hugged her tightly. "Thank you. And I appreciate how you've navigated these troubled waters this past year, and especially how you've found peace these last few months. Watching you has inspired me more than you'll ever know. Have you heard from your birth mother lately?"

Libby glanced around to confirm that most of the congregants had moved toward the door or exited. With no listening ears nearby, her excitement overflowed.

"She lives in Ogdensburg and writes regularly, and her letters are like windows into a hidden world. She shares bits and pieces of her life, such as her love of knitting and the joy she finds in serving at church. Her last letter even told me about her deceased husband, Leonard's father, and how he was the love of her life."

Connie took her hand and squeezed it. "And Leonard? What of him? He came and left so quickly."

"He is well, and happy that he met me, but Mother says he's still grieving. Still bitter from all he lost when his wife and son died. But she prays for both of us every day, and I have begun to pray for both of them every day too. Can you believe, after all these years, I have a whole other family?"

Connie nodded. "It is pretty amazing—and a little confusing, I expect. Do you want to meet your birth mother one day?"

Libby bit her lip for a moment in thought. "At first, I didn't want to. Now, with every successive letter that she signs, *Love,*

Ma, I desire to meet her more and more. So yes, I would love to meet her someday. When she's ready."

Her tone danced with longing and wonder. What would it be like to finally meet her? She'd pondered it for days on end.

Connie's eyes reflected shared emotions, but then they flashed with concern Libby understood all too well. "And what of Owen? He's been gone for three months now. Does he write?"

She sucked in an excited breath, thrilled her friend wanted to know about Owen. Connie had been so dismissive of her feelings before that Libby had avoided the topic with her since. "Owen writes every week. He's working hard at a railroad station to make a future for us and traveling a bit to settle his affairs. I believe he is healing and finding peace too."

Connie smiled, but it didn't rise to her eyes. "Do you love him, Libby? Does he love you? Will he return soon?"

Libby giggled. "Yes, yes, and yes. His letters are filled with sentiments of love and dreams for a future together. Each is an invitation deeper into his world, into his heart. Yet he also begs for patience while he puts things in order. It's as if he's on a journey of self-discovery, as I have been."

As the room grew quiet, Connie slipped her arm into Libby's and led her toward the door. "I'm happy for you, friend. We'd better go so Pastor can get home."

Libby warmed at the support from Connie. It boosted her courage to share the concerns she'd held inside. "I have mixed emotions, though. I'm excited for the love he so freely shares, but what about the personal journey he's taking? In the end, will he choose wealth and status in Canada over village life with me in America?"

Connie stopped them short of the church door. "Trust God, Libby. Remember what Jeremiah 29 says. His plans for you are always the best plans, and if you follow them, He'll give you hope for a bright future—with or without Owen."

Libby sighed. "You're right, of course. Patience. Trust. Hope. Got it."

~

*O*wen hid behind Mr. Montonna and Will in nervous anticipation, waiting for the moment Libby would emerge from the church. The minutes stretched into what felt like eternity, every heartbeat a longing to finally see her. After three long months of soul-searching, settling matters, and finding his purpose, the future was about to unfold.

Will reached behind and tapped Owen on the arm. He sneaked a peek and beheld Libby with Nurse Connie, her smile so radiant it could extinguish the darkest moments of the past few months. His blood surged, rising from his heart, up his neck, and into his face.

Everything in him wanted to rush past Libby's father and brother, sprint to her, and wrap her in a hug, but he fisted his hands, took a deep breath, and waited.

Waited until Libby saw him first.

How would she respond? After months of promises and praying for patience, would she be ready? He'd been on a life-changing voyage that led him to this moment. Had she?

As he waited for her, he marveled at the transformation he'd made. By God's great grace, he'd shed the shadows of sorrow and shame and rejection and found a sense of purpose. He hoped she would share that unfolding adventure with him.

Libby hugged her friend and headed their way, swinging her reticule and humming a hymn. When she noticed her papa and brother, she stopped in her tracks. "What's going on with you two? You both look as though you've swallowed a Cheshire cat."

As if her father and brother were a door to his future, the two stepped aside and revealed Owen. He took two steps forward, his heart racing and wearing a grin so wide, it hurt his face.

He wished he had a camera just then, to capture the magical moment in front of him.

When Libby caught sight of him, her face displayed unbelief that turned to surprise that transformed into awe, reminding him of the dawning of a new day, bursting through the dark night. Her beauty a canvas of soft pinks in her cheeks, golden flecks in her eyes, and a glimmer of pure joy. Her eyes danced with delight, speaking volumes of the emotions exploding inside. In that moment, the uncertainties of what might happen, the weight of the past, and the trials of his journey seemed to dissipate like a mist after a stormy gale.

Her eyes, filled with delight and wonder, locked onto his, and the world around them seemed to fade into the abyss. The silent language of love bridged the gap as time stopped. She closed the distance between them, and to his surprise, Libby began to laugh, loud and free. She didn't even cover her mouth as she always did.

Mr. Montonna joined the joy-filled moment with a hearty chuckle. "Libby, do you mind if we invite this special guest for Thanksgiving dinner?"

The playfulness in his tone caused everyone to join Libby in a bout of merriment. They all waited for Libby to answer, but she stood silent, as if she was mute. After a moment, Alberta touched her arm, tugging Libby from her trance.

Libby curtsied. "Of course, Papa."

What was going on with her? So formal. So quiet. Did she disapprove? Her eyes said otherwise.

The ride back to the lighthouse was filled with chatter from the family about the sermon, the weather, the meal to come. Libby sat next to him but didn't speak. Her silence was confusing at best.

When they arrived home, Alberta's eyes flickered with

fun. "Why don't you two take a walk on this lovely day? I suspect you have a bit of catching up to do. The roast won't be ready for another hour, though nothing further needs done."

Libby's brows furrowed. "If you're sure."

Will answered. "She's sure. I'll help, if needed. Now skedaddle, missy."

Buoy galloped from the barn and almost knocked Owen off balance. "Well, hello, boy. Have you been taking good care of this lovely lass as I asked?"

The dog barked a greeting, and Owen gave him a hearty hug.

Buoy shadowed them, begging attention as Owen led Libby down to the river's edge to the very place they had perched on the rock he'd sat on that fateful night. He'd missed the spot's soothing sight, its unique scent, its pleasant sound. But he had missed Libby so much more.

Her velvety brown, jewel-like eyes flecked with gold. Her two little dimples, hidden until she smiled wide. Her luxurious black hair shimmering in the sun. He couldn't take his eyes off her as he took one of her delicate hands in his own.

She interrupted his adoration of her with a nervous giggle, sweet and childlike. She rubbed Buoy's head as she spoke. "You've come back, but will you stay?"

The gentle breeze, tinged with a touch of autumn, prodded him to answer. "Oh, Libby. I have so much to say. But first, how are you?"

As Libby poured out her heart in what must be a nervous release, Owen savored more than her words. Her voice, transcending the words in her letters. Her face, expressing the joy and peace she had found.

She unfolded her journey to forgiveness, detailing God's gentle nudges and her struggle to submit. But as she disclosed the peace that passed her understanding, her entire countenance reflected the transformation she'd undergone, and it took his breath away.

Eventually, she paused and lifted her hand to her cheek. "For shame! In my surprise and astonishment that you're here, I've run on and on. I want to hear about *you*, Owen. I've waited far too long. Dreamed of it every night. Longed for this moment."

Owen laughed, his heart overflowing at the wonder of it too. The gentle waves lapping against the shore of the St. Lawrence created a calming backdrop for Owen to share his story.

"I've been in Clayton most of the time, but I visited my father twice."

Scratching Buoy's pert ears, Libby gasped. "In Clayton? But that's only hours from here. Why have you not visited?"

Owen kissed her hand, which he refused to release. "I had to find peace, too, Libby, or I'd never be all you would need me to be."

Libby nodded her acceptance, waiting for him to go on.

As he shared the details of his journeys to see his father and settle things with him and Chelsey, the weight of his words was softened by her welcoming attention and frequent head nods. He revealed the complexities of his family dynamics, the difficult moments of standing up to his father as she had done, and the challenges of reconciliation.

"But I did it, Libby. For the first time in my life, thanks to you, I stood up to my father and forced him to hear me out. It wasn't easy, but I did it."

Libby squeezed his hand, then patted it with the other. "It's not easy to confront family. And I'm sure that was daunting with your father. I'm proud of you, Owen."

"I'm not sure if we'll patch things up between us, but at least I've said my piece and pray he finds God's peace."

With a twinkle in his eye, Owen turned to happier stories, painting the picture of his work at the railroad station in

Clayton and, more importantly, learning the newspaper trade in his spare time from an elderly journalist named Mr. Harrington.

"I want to take over the newspaper, but in the meantime, the railroad pays well, and that will give us a start."

Will appeared at the crest of the hill. "Time for dinner, you two. Come and join the family. Let's give thanks and enjoy this hearty meal together."

Buoy hopped up and bolted for the house. Apparently, the word 'dinner' hit its mark.

Owen offered Libby his arm. "Happy Thanksgiving, Libby."

She giggled. "Oh, it's the happiest, Owen."

As they climbed the hilly shore to the cottage, Owen lifted a silent prayer.

Come and join the family?

Oh, may it be so!

CHAPTER 16

The setting sun sparkled on the tips of the gentle waves as the Tibbetts Point Lighthouse beacon spread its band of hope across the water. Such a wonderful Thanksgiving with all the people Libby loved most.

She climbed the tower to enjoy the last rays of the day with Owen and Papa. But her papa suddenly made himself scarce, feigning his need of the outhouse and a fresh cup of coffee. His grin and the sparkle in his eyes took years off his countenance, and she wondered what was behind them.

Libby joined Owen on the lighthouse parapet, tugging her coat a little tighter and leaning her forearms on the rail, joining him to share in the beauty of the setting sun as it danced over the vast expanse of Lake Ontario in the distance and the mighty St. Lawrence in front of them. The close of Thanksgiving Day painted rose, peach, orange, pink, and lilac on puffy clouds, and then over the entire landscape and water beyond.

Golden light followed a large laker that passed near Wolfe Island, while another ship headed out to sea closer to their shore. Soon, the winter's ice would close the shipping channel until the spring thaw, but for now, traffic continued.

She pointed toward the ships. "What must it be like to sail the high seas and explore foreign lands? Such an adventuresome life, I suspect."

Owen drew her to him like the moon draws in the tides, the warmth of his embrace shielding her against the cool evening breeze. "I've done my share of sailing and journeying, and I must say, the only place on earth I want to be is in your arms. That, my wee, darling chickadee, is home."

Her heart fluttered at his words, a sweet mixture of hope and joy welling up within her. He took a step back, his hands grasping hers and knelt on one knee, his baby blues sparkling like the stars popping out above them.

"Libby, you are the anchor of my soul, the light that guides me home. My precious gift from God. Will you make me the happiest man in the world, share the adventures of life with me, and be my wife? I promise, I will cherish you always."

She'd hoped for this moment. Dreamed of it as she'd prayed under starlit skies and whispered wishes for it to the heavens. Her eyes welled with tears as she gazed into Owen's, finding in them warm pools of love. In that twinkle of time, the journey they'd been on, together and apart, flashed through her thoughts. Each day a chapter in the story that had brought them to this magical moment.

A gentle, joyful laugh escaped her lips as a tear sneaked down her cheek. "Mama made me promise that any man who sought my hand would ask Papa's permission first. I have to honor that promise, Owen, so I will give you my answer after you speak to him."

Owen stood and chuckled, kissing the palms of both her hands. "My dear chickadee, I've already done that. While you were chatting with Connie in church, I asked his permission and received it with his blessing. That's why your father has been so accommodating—and your brother, too, especially when I told him about starting our life together in Clayton."

Libby's heart skipped several beats, gratitude and surprise warming her cheeks. "You did?"

Owen gently cupped her face in his hands. He tipped his head in affirmation as he held her tenderly. She never wanted the moment to end. "I wanted your papa's blessing. Your brother's too. I love you, Libby, and I want our marriage to have a firm foundation of respect and trust."

Overwhelmed by Owen's wisdom, she wrapped her arms around him, his hands leaving her face to caress her hair. She whispered, "Thank you for that."

For several moments, they fell silent. He pressed his cheek to her temple, sending her heart skipping like a little girl in a field of dandelions. But she wanted to be closer still, so she settled her cheek on his chest, basking in the heartbeat of the man she loved. The man who would be her husband. In the anticipation and excitement for the journey ahead.

Owen gently pulled her back to gaze into her eyes. "Well? Will you?"

What was he asking? "Will I?"

He blew out a ragged breath. "Marry me, silly lass. Say yes before I burst a blood vessel. Please!"

Foolish girl. She'd nearly spoiled the moment.

"Yes, Owen, a thousand times, yes! I will be honored to be your wife, your companion, and your best friend. Forever and ever!"

Owen's eyes lit up with delight, and he again gathered her into a warm embrace. "Aye, you scared me, Miss Libby. Your heart is my lighthouse. Your arms my safe haven. Your eyes a beacon of hope. If you'd have said no, I don't know what I would have done."

Libby shrugged. "No worries there. I love you and feel the same about you."

She stepped back to catch her breath and took hold of the railing. So many wonderful emotions.

Owen laid his hand on hers, gentle as a feather. "There's an Irish blessing I wish to give us this day. 'To all the days here and after—may they be filled with fond memories, happiness, and laughter.'"

Papa poked his head through the hatch, clambered up the ladder, and entered the light room. "Well now, Mr. Shanahan. Did you ask her yet? I have work to do."

Libby ran to her papa and threw her arms around him. "He did, and he's made me the happiest girl on this earth!" She pulled back to gaze at his face. "So did you, Papa, for agreeing. Thank you."

He kissed her on the top of her head. "You two are a good match. I'm confident that Owen loves you and will take good care of you. Besides, you'll only be a few hours away, and that's a blessing."

"We'll come and see you often, Papa."

Owen joined them. "We promise."

Papa chuckled. "You'd better. Now skedaddle and let me work."

After wishing him well, Libby and Owen descended the tower to walk the grounds. The moonshine bathed the lighthouse in a silvery cloak as the starry sky sparkled its accolades. Dried leaves danced on the breeze.

Owen led her to the swing nestled under the oak, nearly bare of leaves in the crisp autumn air. The creak of the swing filled the silence as she settled her skirts around her, tingling with anticipation.

He leaned in, tucked her scarf tight around her neck, and placed a gentle kiss on her cheek, his warm breath sending shivers down her spine. "Ready?"

She inclined her head, a tiny-girl giggle slipping from her lips. Owen set the swing in motion, and the world blurred around her as she ascended into the night sky. Higher and higher she soared as she kicked at the twinkling stars with pointed toes.

For several minutes, Owen kept pushing her, each gentle thrust carrying her between memories of childhood and adulthood, a delicate bridge where the past merged with hope for the future.

The swing slowed to a gentle sway, and Owen stood behind her with his hand resting on the ropes. She turned to him, moonlight glistening in his soft blue eyes.

"Thank you for being my bridge to our future." She swallowed hard, the implication of it warming her.

Owen leaned closer. "Forever, my love. I'll always be here with and for you, pushing you higher and catching you when you fall."

～

*O*wen guided her off the swing and into his arms. He stroked his fingertip along Libby's jawline, then eased a windblown strand of hair from her face. Her dark lashes framed her eyes enticingly as he touched her bottom lip with the tip of his thumb. Soft. Supple.

"May I, my soon-to-be bride?"

Libby nodded almost imperceptibly.

He touched his lips to hers, imparting his love with all his being. Then he wove his fingers in her hair and gently drew her closer. She responded with arms that wrapped around his middle and tugged him to her. He deepened the kiss with an intensity so powerful he had to stop and breathe.

Moonlight illuminated Libby's beautiful face, and he pressed his lips to hers again. The world around them seemed to fade away, leaving hope for a lifetime of dreams shared by the two of them.

As he pulled away, a gentle smile played on her lips,

reflecting the wonder filling the Thanksgiving evening. "Before it gets too cold and we should go inside, there are things I need to share with you."

Her brows furrowed in curiosity, urging him to continue. She licked her lips as if savoring the kiss, an appropriate segue for his next words.

"Will you indulge me in a poem that I memorized for this moment? It seems so appropriate, for it is how I feel about you. I read Elizabeth Barrett Browning's 'How do I Love Thee?' a few weeks ago and couldn't get it off my heart."

Libby grinned. "That's one of my favorite poems, Owen. Did Alberta tell you?"

He shook his head. "My heart did."

He led her to the edge of the lawn, giving them a clear view of the river. He took a deep breath, savoring the events of the past hour and the moments to come. He lifted his voice and quoted the poem.

> *"How do I love thee? Let me count the ways.*
> *I love thee to the depth and breadth and height*
> *My soul can reach, when feeling out of sight*
> *For the ends of being and ideal grace.*
> *I love thee to the level of every day's*
> *Most quiet need, by sun and candle-light."*

Suddenly, Libby joined him. Their voices blended in harmony, a delicate dance declaring their love and commitment to one another.

> *"I love thee freely, as men strive for right;*
> *I love thee purely, as they turn from praise.*
> *I love thee with the passion put to use*
> *In my old griefs, and with my childhood's faith.*
> *I love thee with a love I seemed to lose*

With my lost saints. I love thee with the breath,
Smiles, tears, of all my life; and, if God choose,
I shall but love thee better after death.'"

When they finished, their eyes locked as the words of the poem lingered in the air, solidifying their betrothal. Libby's face glowed in the moonshine. Was it the same joy as he felt? The same longing? Oh, how he wished they could marry this moment and begin their life together!

Libby shivered, breaking the silence with a tone tender with emotion. "When shall we marry?"

The magic moment faded into the reality of practicality as her question hung in the air.

"It's getting cold. Let's go inside and talk about the details over a hot cup of tea."

She let out a deep sigh, as if sad to end their time alone. "We'd best. I'm sure there's a few slices of pumpkin pie leftover to go with our tea."

He wrapped his arm around her, offering the warmth of his body. "Tea and pie sound perfect."

A return to the familiar cottage he'd recuperated in brought a flood of memories. Only six months ago, he didn't know who he was, and his world had turned upside down. He silently thanked the good Lord for His precious providence as he guided Libby toward the door.

Once inside, cozy warmth dispelled the chill of outside. But inside him, a fire blazed.

When they entered the kitchen, Alberta sat knitting mittens while Buoy slept in the corner on an old wool blanket. Libby's sister-in-law surveyed them for several seconds before chuckling heartily. "I daresay love is a beacon that shines into a soul as bright as this lighthouse does. You two are glowing! When's the wedding?"

Libby giggled. "That's what we need to discuss over a cup of tea and slice of your wonderful pumpkin pie."

Alberta stood and gave them both a hug. "Well, congratulations. I'll leave you to it, then. Besides, I'm plumb worn out. Will and Ralph are already asleep, thank goodness. Have a good evening, and Happy Thanksgiving!"

Owen waved as she left the room. "Happy Thanksgiving to you too."

Libby served slices of pie piled high with whipped cream and poured the tea. They settled into the comfort of the kitchen to talk of the next chapter in their story.

After savoring the sweetness of the pie, Owen set down his fork and took a sip of tea. He took a deep breath, the weight of his choices heavy on his shoulders. Would she agree to be his wife after he shared the challenges they would face?

"Libby, I need to be back for work at the railroad station by two tomorrow. Duty calls, you know? But there are a few things I want to discuss with you."

Her gaze met his, a silent invitation to share his thoughts.

He absentmindedly traced the pattern on the teacup. "I want to give you the world, Libby. But it will be without wealth or status, I'm afraid. Father still holds to his threat to keep me from my inheritance, and I've made peace with that. But that means I'll have to work harder than ever. I'm going to stay working at the railroad station, but also going to take over publishing the *St. Lawrence Beacon*."

He searched her eyes for a flicker of joy for him but found only confusion. "Mr. Harrigan, the owner of the *Beacon*, is giving it up. He's elderly and his eyes are failing, so he's moving to Watertown to be with his son. He has agreed that, if I take on the paper as his publisher for seven years, we will own it free and clear. Isn't that amazing?"

"Really? Your dream of being a journalist will finally come

true?" Her smile that rose all the way up to her eyes eased his angst.

"Aye, Mr. Harrigan will take a percentage of the newspaper profits as payment for the building and equipment. There's a small apartment above the office, where I am staying now, and I was thinking ... what if you and your father come with me to Clayton tomorrow? I want to show you the place, dearest. It may not be the grandest, but it'll be a start for us, a few short blocks from the station. It can be a place where our dreams can begin to take root."

A mix of surprise and concern flickered in Libby's eyes. "Two jobs, Owen? That seems like a lot. When would we see each other?"

He shrugged, taking her hands. "I know it won't be easy. It'll be challenging to work at the station and put out a weekly paper, but I'm willing to do it for us, Libby. For our future and for our children that may come. What do you say, darling? Will you take this journey with me, through all the ups and downs, late nights and early mornings? Do you think we can build a life together with all of this?"

Libby squeezed his hands, her eyes reflecting determination and resolve. "I'm with you in all of it, Owen, for better or for worse. Perhaps I can take in a bit of sewing or work at a shop or something, at least until the children come. I think it will be a grand adventure."

Owen brought her hands to his lips, kissing them tenderly, relieved by her declaration. Like a comforting embrace, her steadfast commitment warmed him. "Thank you, Libby. Knowing you're by my side makes this all the sweeter. I'm sure we'll face challenges and celebrate victories, but we'll do it together."

Libby wiggled in her chair, disengaging their intertwined hands. She took a sip of her tea then stood in front of him, as if she were on a mission. "Shall we go and talk to my father about our excursion to Clayton tomorrow? Perhaps Will might relieve Papa for a few hours so he can rest before we journey?"

Owen tugged her onto his lap. "I've already taken care of that, my love. That's why Will went to bed so early."

Libby giggled. "Why, you little rascal! You've thought of everything, didn't you? But when did you have time to do all that planning and plotting?"

At Owen's self-satisfied chuckle, Buoy stirred from his slumber, indulging in a hearty, exaggerated stretch that prompted more laughter from both of them. Owen clapped a hand over his mouth, hoping they hadn't awakened the family above. He shrugged apologetically, a grin spreading across his face. "When you were helping Alberta with the dishes. What did you think I was doing? Twiddling my thumbs?"

Libby's eyes sparkled in the candlelight. "You never twiddle your thumbs, sir. You're the hardest worker I've ever known. The sweetest servant a woman can have by her side. I am a blessed woman—of that, I am sure."

CHAPTER 17

A week later, Libby stepped into the cold December morning bundled in a heavy woolen coat and her favorite knitted scarf, the last one her mama had made for her. She wrinkled her nose at the accumulating clouds suggesting snow to come. On her birthday, no less.

"Ah, well. Work must go on."

She grasped her woven basket of damp laundry tighter, making her way to the side of the cottage where she'd hang the clothes as quickly as she could. Visible puffs of breath and the crunch of the frosty ground made her question doing laundry on such a day.

But Ralphie was out of diapers, and veering off their Tuesday laundry day could put their tight schedule to the test. Her wedding day was a mere twenty days away, and there was much to do.

"Please, Lord. Help us finish my dress and the details of the wedding and for my move to Clayton. I'm in such a tizzy about it all."

As she hung the laundry, she continued to pray. The wooden pegs creaked with every garment she hung, the cold making her fingers stiff and slow. Halfway through, she paused to blow on her hands and warm them. She glanced heavenward and scowled at the sky, pointing a raw finger at the building clouds. "You hold off and let these things dry."

When she carefully pinned her lacy pantalets to the line, a shiver ran down her spine. What if an unexpected visitor came to wish her happy birthday and saw her unmentionables soaring in the wind? She chuckled at the silliness of embarrassment. She'd soon face much more vulnerable experiences in the days ahead.

When her task was done, she surveyed the laundry dancing and swaying in the breeze. She sighed at the quiet satisfaction in completing such a simple task. How would she do laundry in Clayton? The newspaper office was smack-dab in the center of downtown with no real yard. Her heart lurched.

Perhaps she'd hang laundry in a discreet corner of the apartment? All her chores would change. No more wide-open spaces, cows to milk, eggs to gather, or lighthouse lamps to extinguish. Only the hustle and bustle of village life.

Owen would be bustling, too, with two jobs. But what would she do with all her time? What did God have in store for her?

So many unknowns.

She hurried back to the house where Buoy sat on the porch waiting for her. She let them both in and shut the door against the cold. Removing her coat and scarf, she headed for the kettle. Perhaps a hot cup of tea would warm her and settle her angst.

Buoy took his place in the corner of the kitchen and promptly fell asleep. Oh, how she'd miss her furry friend!

She glanced out the window. She loved the crisp, fresh air of Tibbetts Point. The rhythm of the light's motion at night. The hoot of the owls and howl of the coyotes. The joys of daily life with her family.

She poured a steaming cup of tea and warmed her fingers over it before taking a sip. In only twenty days, everything would change. But before she rested, she needed to write an invitation. She went into the parlor, sat at the writing desk, and began to compose a missive for her birth mother and half brother in Ogdensburg.

Dearest Mother and Leonard,

I hope this letter finds you in good health and high spirits. It is with great joy and anticipation that I invite you into a new chapter of my life.

On the twenty-fourth day of December in the year of our Lord 1894 at ten o'clock, I shall be joined in holy matrimony to my beloved, Martin Owen Shanahan. The ceremony will take place in Cape Vincent.

As I prepare to embark on the journey into matrimony, your presence would be a cherished gift, and I extend this invitation with an open heart, hoping the Lord will guide you to join me on this special day.

With love and anticipation,

Elizabeth Eliza Montonna

Libby sealed the letter and stamped it with care. Tomorrow, she would trek into town and send it on its way.

Alberta descended the staircase and met Libby on her way to the kitchen. "That boy wiggles in his sleep. It's almost eleven, and he refused to go down until he passed out from exhaustion. If only we could borrow a bit of that energy, we'd have your wedding gown finished and a whole new trousseau to boot."

Libby chuckled at her sister-in-law as she refilled her teacup. A year from now, would she have a baby of her own? The thought made her stomach do a flip. "Alberta, what was it like to leave your family and all you knew, marry Will, move here, and soon be with child? I never realized what a huge change that must have been for you."

Alberta poured a cup of tea and sat next to her. The twinkle in Alberta's eyes settled her fears. "It was like stepping into a completely different world. It reminded me of *Alice's Adventure in Wonderland*. Leaving Mother and Father and everything behind was like going down a rabbit hole into an unexpected— and at times scary—world. But the love we share and the joy of family makes it all worth it. It's an adventure I wouldn't trade for anything."

Libby touched her arm. "I'm sorry I didn't help you on that journey. I had no idea. You're like the big sister I never had, and now that Mama's gone, you're the woman I trust most. Will you guide me in this journey, please?"

Alberta reached over and hugged her. "Of course, I will. We'll be only a few hours apart, and we can write letters. I'll always be here for you, Libby."

Libby smiled. She'd miss her daily chats with Alberta, but perhaps she'd make new friends in Clayton. She'd simply have to trust God for all of it. "Thank you for that."

Alberta took a sip of her tea. "And today you are twenty-one. Happy birthday, Libby. I have a special surprise for you for dinner. Until then, shall we work on your wedding dress?"

To the comforting tick of Mama's clock on the parlor mantel, Libby and Alberta worked on her dress, a sense of peace filling the room. The soft rustle of yards of delicate fabric, needles, and threads echoed the coming of this new chapter of her life.

A distant clatter of hooves interrupted her sewing, drawing her gaze out the window. "Goodness! And on such a blustery day. Can it be?"

"Who is it, Libby?"

As if she'd seen St. Nick himself, Libby clapped and let out a high-pitched squeal. "Quick. Put away all this sewing. He can't see my wedding dress."

"Who, Libby? Who can't see?"

"It's Owen! Hurry!"

Libby scooped up the fabric and ran it upstairs, while Alberta put the thread and needles and scissors back into the sewing basket. Thank heavens they hadn't laid out the lace and embellishments.

Buoy followed her to the door, tail wagging eagerly.

Her heart pounded with surprise and excitement as she threw on her coat to greet her beloved, rushing out the door. "Owen! You've come. You'll catch your death out here."

He'd already dismounted and tethered his horse, so he rushed to wrap her in a warm embrace, ignoring the dog. When he drew back, his eyes sparkled with delight, his cheeks rosy as Santa's. Indeed, no one could bring a better gift.

He placed a tender kiss on her forehead. "Happy birthday, my darling Libby!"

Though she wanted to linger alone with him, a gust of cold wind sent them inside. He bent down to rub Buoy's head as Alberta met them at the door.

"Welcome, Owen. Why don't you two sit in the parlor until dinner? Papa and Ralph are asleep. Will is upstairs reading, but I'll have him shelter your horse."

Owen shook his head. "Nae. I can do it. I wanted to warm up a bit first."

She was already partway up the steps before responding. "No, no. Will shall be glad to see you."

Libby led Owen to the settee, where she stole a hug and kissed him on the cheek. Perhaps she'd snatch a longer kiss later.

Owen gave Buoy a proper welcome. "Hello, my furry friend. Have you been keeping an eye on this one?"

The mirth that emanated from Owen filled her heart to overflowing.

"What a surprise!" Will, interrupted the moment, almost running down the stairs and putting his hand out to Owen. "Welcome. Get warm. I'll tend to your horse."

He did, and Alberta brought a tray of tea and shortbread. "Enjoy the quiet. When Ralph wakes, it's all over."

Libby grinned. "Thank you. Sure I can't help?"

"Absolutely not. I forbid you from coming into the kitchen until dinner. After all, it's your birthday."

Owen touched the tip of her nose with his forefinger. "Yes, it is. Thank you, Alberta."

For almost an hour, Libby and her betrothed reveled in stories and laughter, soaking in the joy of being together, the forgotten laundry swaying in the cold December air and her faithful dog sleeping at her feet.

"Thank you for your frequent and interesting letters, Owen. When I read them, I realize what a wonderful journalist you'll be. The news you share—and how you make me picture each moment—shows me that your readers will love your stories as much as I do."

Owen's eyes sparked under her affirmation. "And I thank you for your returning missives to me. Each one is a lifeline across the distance."

Libby snuggled closer to him. "And soon, there will no longer be distance between us."

～

Owen basked in the warmth of the Montonna home where love and care formed the foundation. Aye, that's exactly what he wanted for Libby and himself.

Alberta broke into his musings with an announcement and a job. "Dinner's ready! Libby, will you please get Ralph and wake Papa? Owen, would you fetch Will, please? I expect he's in the barn."

Once greetings were made and everyone sat around a table set with their best tableware, Alberta served the birthday meal. Roast chicken, mashed potatoes with her delicious gravy, and this past season's canned carrots and beans. And of course, her famous sourdough bread with plenty of freshly churned butter.

Papa gave thanks and waved his arms like a band conductor. "Eat up, everyone!"

Conversation flowed effortlessly with stories of Libby's childhood and plans for the wedding.

When the meal was done, Alberta returned from the pantry with a huge grin, placing a beautifully decorated cake in the center, a sweet token of celebration for Libby's twenty-first birthday.

Everyone wished Libby a wonderful day and entire year with so much affection that a lump formed in Owen's throat. His birthday celebrations had been nothing but social events bent on bringing business to his father.

She beamed around the table. "Thank you, Alberta. Owen. Everyone. This is the best birthday ever!"

Will chuckled, clicking his tongue. "Better than the birthday you got your new pony? Owen tops that?"

Libby giggled, covering her mouth with a napkin. "Way better!"

Papa held his fork in midair, a piece of cake speared on it. "Seriously, Owen. We're happy you're here. You are always welcome, no matter the time or circumstance. You are family now and forever."

Overwhelmed by their acceptance, Owen simply bobbed his head in thanks. For several minutes, he stayed silent, enjoying the banter between father and son, the tenderness between mother and baby, and most of all, the birthday girl's overflowing joy.

Eventually, Owen shared tales of the bustling railroad station and the lively village of Clayton, the details of overly imperious rich women in fur coats and nannies herding children like shepherds making everyone smile.

"But it's much quieter from now until May. The cottagers and island-dwellers have closed up their summer homes and headed back to the cities where they reside. There are now only about forty-four hundred year-round folks in Clayton."

Will shrugged. "That's about three times the population of Cape Vincent, so I expect it'll feel like a large metropolitan city to my sister."

Libby sent him a scolding frown. "Stuff and nonsense. I'm made of sterner stuff than you'll ever admit and will employ it well, brother."

The eruption of laughter warmed Owen's heart, another element of life that would surely add to their newly married life.

The afternoon flew by in the midst of shared dreams and whispered secrets, surrounded by the comforting presence of Libby's family slipping in and out of the parlor. They enjoyed a sweet time playing with wee Ralph, sparking excitement and a silent prayer for he and Libby to enjoy their own children one day.

Then Libby's father joined them in the cozy parlor, and sat near them, his face serious. "Children, now is as good a time as any to share my lessons on love. Marriage is a lot like tending a lighthouse."

Libby smiled as Owen leaned in to learn all he could. Since his father had never spoken into his life, save discouragement, he longed for a man like Mr. Montonna to share his knowledge.

"Like a lightkeeper keeps the lamp burning, marriage requires much work. It's not always easy, and you'll need to trim the wick, replenish the oil, and ensure the light always stays bright. But there's deep satisfaction in sharing that responsibility."

Libby dipped her chin. "Just as I always enjoyed working with you, Papa."

A small smile played on his lips, his eyes twinkling. "Exactly. And much as the keeper tends to the flame, you two must nurture the flame of love. Keep it alive with patience, kindness, and much laughter."

Owen absorbed the wisdom of his words. "We will, Mr. Montonna. I promise."

Libby's father stiffened, and he waved off Owen's comment as if he were offended by it. "Enough with 'Mr. Montonna.' Call me 'Papa.' You are family."

Owen pulsed with joy. He had a family, even if his own father had chosen to disown him.

Papa's gaze shifted to the window and then back to them. "Remember, it's not always clear skies and calm seas. There will be times when the waves crash against the rocks and fog hides the way forward. That's when you two must stand strong, united, immovable, a light in each other's darkness. Be a constant source of support and strength that will help you weather any storm together and be a beacon for all you meet."

Libby's hands trembled. "We will, Papa."

The clock chimed four times, tugging Owen from that sacred moment. "Goodness! I best be on my way. Thank you for those words of wisdom. I will tuck them deep in my heart and make them a part of our life together. And I promise I will take good care of your daughter."

Papa playfully wagged a finger at him. "You better, son, or I'll take a switch to your backside."

That dispelled the somber tone of the conversation and allowed the three of them to enjoy a hearty laugh together.

"I'll leave you to say goodbye to your bride-to-be, and I'll see you at the wedding. Godspeed, son."

Papa stood and gave him a warm embrace before exiting the room, leaving him alone with Libby.

"Your papa is an amazing man, Libby. Mine would never share such counsel."

"Perhaps one day, your father will become the man you hope him to be. Don't give up on praying for him."

"I won't. But now, may I have a goodbye kiss, my love?" His voice carried a gentle plea.

Libby fluttered her lashes, the room quiet with only the tick of the clock and his heart beating strong and steady. He touched her hair, its silky strands bringing comfort.

But before he could kiss her, she pressed her lips to his, a sweet, lingering caress that promised love deep and tender. When she moved back, she giggled. "I've wanted to do that all afternoon." She covered her mouth at the admission, her cheeks growing a lovely pink.

"Me, too," he admitted, and met her lips with his one more time. Then, he playfully pecked the tip of her nose, each rosy cheek, and her forehead. "Until we meet again, that should hold you."

Owen hung on the kisses, the words, the joy, the beauty of family all the way back to Clayton. Indeed, he cherished every moment of the day and anticipated many to come as he surveyed the small apartment that would become their home. He was grateful Mr. Harrigan had kindly relinquished the space and left his modest furnishings as a start for their future.

His heart brimming with hope and trepidation, Owen picked up his pen to compose a letter—to his father.

Dear Father,

I trust this letter finds you well. As I approach my wedding day with Libby, I reflect on our stormy relationship, and I pray for peace. The bonds that connect us as father and son are from our

Creator, no matter our differences. I wish to extend an olive branch, to mend what is broken, and to rebuild the bridge that connects us.

Libby and I will be wed on the twenty-fourth day of December in Cape Vincent at ten in the morning. Your presence would warm my heart and honor our sacred union. It would mean the world to me if you would accept this invitation to celebrate with us. It is my earnest desire to find reconciliation with you.

Wishing you well as I hope for a future with you, my father,
Owen

He sealed the letter and placed it with Libby's, praying the two missives would reach their destinations and bear fruit that would bring life.

EPILOGUE

*A*s Libby prepared for the day, her heart soared with the pink, blue, and yellow cotton-candy clouds billowing outside her window. The early-morning sun painted the sky in hues of soft pastels, casting a warm glow on snow-covered Tibbetts Point. A perfect Christmas Eve morning for a wedding.

Her wedding day!

Within hours, she'd be leaving her childhood home, the beacon of hope that had guided her through two decades of life. She would soon exchange this magical place for wonders and adventures of married life in the village of Clayton.

She donned her newly made wedding gown fashioned with fondness and much conversation between Alberta and herself, even as they rather frantically sewed every detail. The dress was beyond her wildest dreams. The stuff of a fairy story.

She bit back tears, thanking the Lord for His providence and provision. He had delivered Owen onto her shore and into her heart, and soon they would be wed. What a gift!

Alberta entered the room, straightened the delicate lace around her shoulders, and patted her hair. "Your dress is perfect, Libby, and we finished it in the nick of time."

SUSAN G MATHIS

Libby grabbed her hand. "Thank you, sister. I cherish every inch of it."

"And you'll adore your hair, too, when I'm finished with it. I borrowed Connie's curling tongs, and she showed me how to use them."

She worked Libby's locks into a soft updo with fashionable and gentle waves. Then she added a hint of tendrils around her nape.

Libby held the small hand mirror up to inspect it and gasped. "Oh, Alberta. It's enchanting!"

"Sit still, girl, and let me attach the veil." Her sister-in-law kissed her on the cheek and set the delicate lace veil on top of her head, pinning it securely. Once done, Alberta plucked her up to stand and observed from head to toe.

In the timeless tradition of the day, Libby felt a vision of elegance and grace in the ivory satin draped modestly over her. She ran a hand over her high bodice, embellished with lace and beads, and smoothed her full skirt.

Alberta fluffed her puffy sleeves and grinned. "Perfect! Exquisite! And now, for your gift." She handed Libby a brown paper package wrapped with a white satin ribbon.

When Libby opened it, she gasped. An impeccable needlepoint read, *To all the days here and after—may they be filled with fond memories, happiness, and laughter.*

"Thank you, sister. It will grace our home always. But how did you know this Irish blessing was special to Owen and me?"

Alberta chuckled. "I have ears, girl. You told me about it the day after you were betrothed, and I've been working on it since."

Libby tittered. "Oh, I forgot. Thank you so much. You must have worked day and night to finish it."

A knock on the door interrupted them. "May I come in, please?" Papa entered, dressed in his Sunday best. "Goodness! You are captivating, my lovely daughter, as I knew you would

184

be. Well done, Alberta. May I have a moment alone with Libby, please?"

Alberta smiled, pressing a blue lacy handkerchief into Libby's hand. "Something borrowed and blue." She fled the room, closing the door gently.

Papa chuckled softly, his hands behind his back as if hiding a surprise.

Libby stood in bittersweet anticipation, her heart overflowing and her mind racing with joy, excitement, and a touch of sadness. "Thank you, Papa, for everything. I can't imagine not living here, not being with you every day. I will miss you."

"I will miss you, too, but you'll not be far away. I have a gift for you. Something old and something new." He held out his hand.

"Mama's pearls? I couldn't. They are far too valuable." A small whimper escaped her lips.

Silently, Papa wrapped them around her neck and clasped them securely. Three long strands draped over her dress, adding the perfect finishing touch. He patted her shoulders. "Mama wanted you to have them. And the other?" He pulled an envelope from his pocket and handed it to her. "There are a few crisp new bills in there, but you know I don't write well, so I'd call a letter from me something new, eh?"

She received the envelope from him, but instead of opening it, she wrapped her arms around him and hugged him. "I love you, Papa."

He patted her back but gently separated from her. "I love you, too, darling. We leave for the church in ten minutes. Best be ready."

When he left, she quickly opened the envelope, set aside the four bills, and read his words. Though his penmanship was difficult to decipher, she treasured every word.

My dearest Libby,

Today is a day I have envisioned since the moment you came into my life. A day when you, my precious daughter, embark on a new chapter. Watching you grow into the amazing woman you are today has been the greatest joy of my life, and I'm only sad that your mama isn't here to see it in person. You have blossomed into a woman of grace, strength, and compassion, and you make me proud beyond words.

I give you both my blessings, my guidance, and my unwavering support. May your days be filled with joy, your nights with peace, and your years with love. Cherish every sunrise and sunset, and find joy in small moments and strength to meet the challenges ahead.

All my love,

Papa

What a precious gift! Once she dried her tears and blew her nose, Libby pinched her cheeks and ran her fingers over the pearls. Mama would be here, in spirit, close to her heart.

She gathered her things, donned her coat, and left the cottage, giving Buoy a farewell caress. "I'll see you soon, my friend. Be good."

With that, she stood for a moment on the porch admiring the view, the crisp air carrying the scent of pine and excitement. Like the mighty lighthouse she loved so much, she'd be strong and steadfast, too, no matter what. She was ready to embrace the journey ahead.

～

From behind the altar, Owen surveyed the quaint stone church adorned with wreaths and flickering candles. Family and friends filled the pews, their whispered conversations creating a soft hum as they waited for the service to start. To the right, about halfway down, Dr. Renicks sat with his wife. In front of them, Connie watched for the ceremony to begin with baby Ralph sleeping on her lap.

Wait! There, in the back of the church, Leonard sat staring at the front, serious as usual. Beside him, a woman who resembled Libby caught his eye as well as the eyes of those around her. Libby's birth mother—with a warm smile radiating joy.

Libby would be so pleased.

Owen smoothed his finely tailored suit as he waited in the chancel behind the altar. The church bells pealed forth, alerting the entire village that their nuptials were to commence. His blood surged through his veins, warming him from his heart to his fingertips. He lifted a silent prayer. The organ music filled the air as he took a deep breath, his heart pounding in his chest.

"It's time. Congratulations, Owen." Will gave him an encouraging nod, offered Alberta—Libby's matron of honor— his arm, and the three of them stepped to the front of the altar.

In moments, the woman of Owen's dreams, his future, would join him.

The old doors at the back of the church slowly creaked open, and there she was—Libby, radiant in her elegant wedding gown, escorted by her father. She clutched a bouquet of winter blooms.

Owen swallowed the lump in his throat and blinked back moisture welling up in his eyes. Never, in all his upper-class experiences, university events, or extravagant travels, had he seen anything so beautiful.

The congregation stood as Libby and her father walked down the aisle, and his nerves took flight, firing with excitement, joy, trepidation, and pleasure all at the same time. And then, she was at his side, a glowing, dazzling gift of God. She offered him a shy smile through her veil, and it was all he needed to shore up his shaking knees.

As the ceremony began, no one but Libby, himself, and the

minister mattered. Not Will or Alberta. Not her papa or Libby's birth mother. Not a church full of people. He kept his eyes forward, listening to the minister until the man stopped and glanced at Libby's father before shifting his attention back to them.

"Owen and Elizabeth, God is every man's—and every marriage's—lighthouse. He shines the light of truth, hope, and love. Neither darkness, gale, nor fog can overcome His beacon of hope. At times, He allows storms, so we look to the lighthouse to be rescued. Make that the foundation of your marriage."

When he prompted them to exchange vows, Owen faced Libby, and he couldn't help but smile. The words of love flowed from his heart, and Libby's eyes filled with tears as she said hers. When the minister pronounced them husband and wife, the congregation erupted in applause, and he presented them as a married couple.

As they walked down the aisle, Libby suddenly noticed Leonard—and her birth mother. She let out a gasp and leaned close to him. "They're here. Mother and Leonard are here!"

He grinned so wide, it almost hurt. The pieces of her life's puzzle were coming together beautifully.

When they got to the back of the church, Libby tugged him toward her mother and brother instead of greeting other guests. "We have to meet them, Owen."

He happily complied.

Libby's mother spoke first, tears glistening her eyes, mirroring her daughter's. "Thank you for inviting me, Libby. This is beautiful, and so are you. And I hope you don't mind that I brought two special people with me. This is your Aunt Emma, my sister, who recently married the Rock Island Lighthouse keeper. And this is your cousin, Julia Collins, whose father, Oliver, was my brother. Julia lives at Sister's Island Lighthouse."

Libby smiled. "On the contrary. I'm overjoyed to meet family!"

He and Libby greeted the three women. Then, Libby's mother wrapped her daughter in a warm embrace, so Owen turned to her brother, allowing the holy moment of reunion to take place between them alone.

He greeted Leonard. "Thanks for coming, and Happy Christmas."

Leonard nodded, a tentative grin disappearing as he pressed a letter into his hand. "A man came in right after Libby and stood behind us for the entire ceremony. When the minister pronounced you married, he quickly gave me this and said, 'Give this to Owen. I have urgent business to attend to.'"

Owen assessed the familiar script. *To Martin and Elizabeth.*

Father?

He held the letter to his chest, his heart beating as hard as it had minutes ago. "Thank you, Leonard. If you'll excuse me."

He hurried to the window and scanned the street. Father was nowhere to be seen, so he opened the letter and read it.

Son and his bride,

I accept your olive branch and congratulate you both on your nuptials. As a wedding gift, I have paid Mr. Harrington for the St. Lawrence Beacon. *You now own the building and business free and clear. It won't make you wealthy, but it's a start for you both.*

Father

Could it be true? He swiped the tears that refused to hide. Tears of joy and peace and reconciliation.

Libby joined him, slipping her hand in his. "What's wrong, Owen? Are you all right?"

He chuckled. "Read this."

Libby *ooh*ed and *ahh*ed and gasped as she read the short missive. "He was here?"

Owen sighed, planting a kiss on her forehead. "Everyone was here, Libby. And all is well."

In that moment, as they stood together basking in all God gave them, the lighthouse in the distance seemed to symbolize not only a guiding light but also the enduring strength of family, forgiveness, and hope. Surrounded by the love of their past and present, they prepared to embark a new journey.

Together.

The End

Did you enjoy this book? We hope so!
**Would you take a quick minute to leave a review where you
purchased the book?**
It doesn't have to be long. Just a sentence or two telling what
you liked about the story!

Receive a FREE ebook and get updates when new Wild Heart
books release: https://wildheartbooks.org/newsletter

ABOUT THE AUTHOR

Susan G Mathis is an international award-winning, multi-published author of stories set in the beautiful Thousand Islands, her childhood stomping ground in upstate NY. Susan has been published more than thirty times in full-length novels, novellas, and non-fiction books. She has twelve in her fiction line including, *The Fabric of Hope: An Irish Family Legacy, Christmas Charity, Katelyn's Choice, Devyn's Dilemma, Sara's Surprise, Reagan's Reward, Colleen's Confession, Peyton's Promise, Rachel's Reunion, Mary's Moment,* and *A Summer at Thousand Island House. Libby's Lighthouse* is the first in a three-book lighthouse series coming out in 2024. Her book awards include three Illumination Book Awards, four American Fiction Awards, three Indie Excellence Book Awards, five

Literary Titan Book Awards, a Golden Scroll Award, and a Selah Award.

Before Susan jumped into the fiction world, she served as the Founding Editor of *Thriving Family* magazine and the former Editor/Editorial Director of twelve Focus on the Family publications. Her first two published books were nonfiction. *Countdown for Couples: Preparing for the Adventure of Marriage* with an Indonesian and Spanish version, and *The ReMarriage Adventure: Preparing for a Life of Love and Happiness*, have helped thousands of couples prepare for marriage. Susan is also the author of two picture books, *Lexie's Adventure in Kenya* and *Princess Madison's Rainbow Adventure*. Moreover, she is published in various book compilations including five *Chicken Soup for the Soul* books, *Ready to Wed, Supporting Families Through Meaningful Ministry, The Christian Leadership Experience,* and *Spiritual Mentoring of Teens*. Susan has also written several hundred published magazine and newsletter articles.

Susan is president of American Christian Fiction Writers-CS (ACFW), former vice president of Christian Authors Network (CAN), a member of Christian Independent Publishing Association (CIPA), and a regular writer's contest judge. For over twenty years, Susan has been a speaker at writers' conferences, teachers' conventions, writing groups, and other organizational gatherings. Susan makes her home in Colorado Springs and enjoys traveling around the world but returns each summer to the islands she loves. Visit www.Susan-GMathis.com for more.

ACKNOWLEDGMENTS

To Judy Keeler, my wonderful historical editor, who combs through my manuscripts for accuracy. Because of her, you can trust that my stories are historically correct. And to Salley Williams at Tibbetts Point Lighthouse, who made sure the lighthouse information was accurate.

To my wonderful beta team—Judy, Laurie, Donna, Barb, Melinda, Davalynn, and Mary Alice—who inspire me with your kindness, faithfulness, and wisdom. Thanks for all your hard work and wise input.

To my amazing publisher, Misty Beller, and rock-star editor, Denise Weimer. Thanks to you, I'm soaring on the wings of my writing journey.

And to all my dear friends who have journeyed with me in my writing. Thanks for your emails, social media posts, and especially for your reviews. Most of all, thanks for your friendship.

And to God, from whom all good gifts come. Without You, there would never be a dream or the ability to fulfill that dream. Thank You!

AUTHOR'S NOTE

I hope you enjoy *Libby's Lighthouse*. If you've read any of my other books, you know that I love introducing history to my readers through fictional stories. I hope this story sparks interest in our amazing past, especially the fascinating past of the marvelous Thousand Islands.

Tibbetts Point Lighthouse and the Montonna family are real, though Libby and Owen are fashioned in my imagination, and the real Mrs. Montonna didn't die in 1893 but lived a good, long life. Please note that some of the timing is a little different than the historic record as I took a bit of creative license in bringing this story to life.

This is the first of three lighthouse stories, and I hope you'll enjoy them all. In the series, you'll meet the Row family women —Libby, Julia, and Emma—as they navigate the isolation, danger, and hope for lasting love at three different St. Lawrence River lighthouses. In book two, *Julia's Joy*, you'll experience life at Sister Island Lighthouse, and in book three, *Emma's Engagement*, you'll enjoy the famous Rock Island Lighthouse.

Visit www.SusanGMathis.com/fiction for more information.

Don't miss the next book in the Love at a Lighthouse Series!

Julia's Joy

Chapter 1

As the boat cut through the choppy waves, Julia Collins couldn't help but resent the place that would imprison her for the entire summer, thanks to Granny's wishes and the will that held her future in the balance. The elusive prize of a hefty inheritance dangled around her neck like a heavy golden chain, demanding her sacrifice.

She shifted in her seat to see little but water and an island in the distance. Her discontent matched the chilly, churning water around her as the boat sailed closer to Sister Island Lighthouse. Strung together like pearls on a bracelet, its three tiny islets were miles from her Canadian mainland home, and more than a mile from the New York shore, smack dab in the middle of nowhere in the mighty St. Lawrence River.

Perched on the eastern edge of the island, the lighthouse cottage appeared rather quaint from a distance. Its stone façade and steeply pitched roof hinted at a simpler life, one far removed from the lively city parties, the bustling shopping area, and the vibrant gaggle of people she thrived on. The charm of the cottage, however, only intensified her sense of imprisonment. Even the lighthouse tower, poking out of the center of the house, mocked her arrival.

What was she going to do there all summer? She'd been looking forward to lively romps about town with her friends, but now...this?

Why, Granny? Why?

As the boat docked, Julia reluctantly stepped onto the island, her distain echoing in the hollow clack of her shoes on the wooden planks.

She pressed a few coins into the boatman's hand as he unloaded her luggage, including her easel and art supplies. "Thank you, sir, for the ride. Have a safe journey home."

The stocky old sailor tipped his cap. "You're welcome, miss. Good day."

Julia sucked in a steadying breath. This barren piece of the world would be her new home for months?

Her new home held little to commend it. Concrete-and-rock break walls and cement walkways connected the three islets. And there were no other buildings besides the cottage and an old boathouse and shed. That was all...for miles and miles. It was as if the island itself conspired to keep her within its narrow boundaries, far from the exciting life she'd known and still craved.

Her heart raced as it had when a swarm of wasps had chased her last summer. Her skin prickled, but she steeled herself to endure the days ahead.

Mrs. Dodge, her granny's friend whom she hadn't seen since the funeral, awaited her at the edge of the lawn waving her welcome. A dozen steps beyond her stood a man around Julia's age—her son, whom Julia had met briefly at the funeral. The older woman's eyes shone with a mixture of pity and sympathy, and her smile faltered, making Julia's stomach churn.

Ahead of her lay a summer sentence of solitude—but she couldn't deny that part of this banishment was her own fault, a consequence of her own foolish actions.

Mrs. Dodge cleared her throat, tugging her from her troubles. "Welcome to Sister Island Lighthouse. Come. I have soup on the stove and tea to chase the chill of travel away."

Julia nodded, picking up her valise of her most precious possessions, her art supplies and easel. She steeled herself to face the long, looming days ahead. She could do this. She had no choice but to do this—and endure until the end.

Julia pasted on a smile and squared her shoulders. "Thank you, Mrs. Dodge. I'm Julia Collins, Maybelle Collins's granddaughter."

Mrs. Dodge swiftly took Julia's easel. "I remember, dearie, and I'm sorry for your loss. But I'm happy to see we will have an artist in residence." Before Julia could respond, Mrs. Dodge turned to her son. "William, make your way down here and help with these bags, please. You're not a statue, my boy."

In a flash, the man leaped into motion. Swift as a gazelle, he joined his mother and herself, grabbing hold of Julia's bulkier bags. But before heading toward the cottage, he paused and fixed his assessment of her. What thoughts were running through his mind? She couldn't discern, so she took a moment to size him up as well.

Mrs. Dodge's son, the lightkeeper, possessed a striking physical presence, and his tall, sturdy frame hinted at strength and dignity. His eyes were a soothing shade of blue, the color of the river on a calm day, his strong brow and thin lips adding an intriguing contrast. His thick, coffee-brown hair curled around his ears, framing his face, and long, dark lashes accentuated the reflection of the river in his undiscernible stare.

Despite his handsome features, a scowl adorned his expression, giving an air of mystery and uncertainty to his demeanor. With a subtle shake of his head, the lightkeeper exuded an inhospitable aura, as if safeguarding a hidden secret amid the desolation of the island.

Mrs. Dodge playfully shook a finger at her son. "Hold on a second, young man. Where are your manners? Extend a cordial greeting to our guest, and a smile wouldn't hurt either. After all, she'll be a part of our family for the entire summer."

He seemed to be suppressing a huff. "I'm Lightkeeper Dodge. Welcome." His voice remained monotone and guarded. He didn't smile.

Mrs. Dodge clicked her tongue. "Call him William. Everyone else does."

Julia masked a grin and curtsied. Mrs. Dodge might be petite, but she certainly was spirited. "Thank you, Mrs. Dodge. William."

Once mother and son nodded their acknowledgement, Julia followed Mrs. Dodge to the cottage with William bringing up the rear. As she did, the majestic presence of the lighthouse on Sister Island arrested her attention. The gray limestone structure stood proudly against the backdrop of the river landscape. The two-story dwelling and attached light tower created a harmonious union, blending seamlessly with the natural surroundings.

Stepping nearer, Julia marveled at the meticulous craftsmanship evident in every detail. Her architect father would have appreciated such skillful artistry, may he rest in peace. Proudly recalling the architectural designs her father often shared with her, Julia grinned. The intricate knowledge he'd taught her flooded her mind, and a spark of inspiration ignited within.

The foundation, composed of limestone blocks, merged with the rugged rock outcropping, grounding the entire structure. Beautifully dressed limestone adorned the building, giving it an air of timeless elegance. Julia marveled at the decorative trusses and brackets adorning each end of the gabled roof, hinting at elements of stick-style architecture. Heavy limestone lintels and sills framed the lighthouse's many windows, adding to its sturdiness and charm. Her father's love of architecture served her well.

She admired the tower rising from the northern center of the roof, creating a captivating silhouette. The corbeled stonework beneath the additional story of the ten-sided lantern room added a touch of sophistication to the structure. As she rounded the east side of the house, she glimpsed two inset gable dormers in the steeply pitched southern roof.

Perhaps she could capture the essence of this place on canvas. Maybe, just maybe, with each stroke of her paintbrush, she could transform this banishment into something beautiful. Maybe then, this desolate place wouldn't be so bad.

She shifted from one foot to another, considering from what angle she might sketch the house. Perhaps, with the long days ahead, she'd paint several versions of it.

The cottage exuded a sense of history and purpose, as if the lighthouse itself held the tales of countless journeys along the river. Julia lingered for another moment, taking in the details of the guardian of the river and the symbol of resilience against the elements.

Mrs. Dodge pulled her from her musings. "Are you coming, dear?"

Startled, Julia hurried to join her on the steps of the porch that led to the one-story addition on the eastern side of the cottage. "I'm sorry. I was admiring your lighthouse. It is beautiful, Mrs. Dodge."

The woman chuckled as she held open a screen door. "It is, rather. And since you'll be a part of the family, you can call me Aunt Dee. It's less formal. Come into the kitchen and sit a spell."

Julia followed her into the sunny kitchen and set her valise on the counter. "Thank you. May I use your privy, please?"

Aunt Dee nodded, pointing toward the door. "Of course. It's outside, in the shed next to the boathouse."

Julia thanked her, and she stepped back outside. The wooden shed, a modest abode for a bathroom, bore the marks of time and weather, the paint having faded into subtle hues.

Goodness! An outside privy would be quite a change from her grandmother's fine indoor plumbing. Another aspect of her banishment.

Julia approached the entrance, her footsteps accompanied by the soft crunch of gravel. As she opened the door, a mixture of mustiness and the scent of aged wood accosted her. The interior revealed a functional yet compact space. A small window allowed slivers of natural light to filter in, diffusing to illuminate the vintage fixtures and turquoise patina of well-worn surfaces within. Against one wall, a shelf held neatly arranged supplies—buckets, cleaning tools, an old Sears catalogue and newspapers, an oil lamp, and other essentials.

When she returned to the cottage, a bowl of steaming vegetable soup and fresh bread awaited her. Aunt Dee motioned for her to sit. "After we eat, I'll show you your room and the rest of the cottage. This place may not be what you're used to, but I hope it'll do for a summer on the island."

It would have to do if she was to get her inheritance. "Thank you for having me. My grandmother spoke so highly of you and the beauty of the river."

William tore a few pieces off the heel of bread and plopped

it into his soup. "Your grandmother was correct. It's wonderful here."

The meal continued with stilted small talk that refused to settle her. Aunt Dee chattered about small things that mattered little to Julia. William barely said a word, eying her undiscernibly. She couldn't imagine an entire summer of this, and she already missed the city gossip. Would every meal be this awkward? If so, she'd suffer from indigestion daily.

When they were done, Aunt Dee stood and set her bowl in the sink. "William, please clear the table while I show Julia her room."

He nodded, picking up his dish. "Happy to. Thanks for lunch." He caught Julia's eye, a half smile gracing his lips.

Perhaps he'd thaw sooner rather than later? She hoped so.

Julia picked up her valise of art supplies and followed Aunt Dee up the narrow staircase to a tiny hallway. Three doors and another staircase fed off of it. Aunt Dee motioned toward each room. "This is my room, William's room, and your room. The stairs lead to the lighthouse tower." She opened the second door on the right. "I hope you like it. The dormer gives you a lovely view of the main channel and New York beyond."

The small room held only a single bed, dresser, and small desk with a chair. But Aunt Dee was correct. The view was spectacular. "It's lovely. Thanks again for hosting me."

Aunt Dee waved a dismissive hand. "Stuff and nonsense. No hosting to it. You're family now. Get settled and have a rest. I'll be downstairs if you need anything."

Julia set her case on the desk and plunked down on the bed, heaving a weary sigh. It was beautiful out here, to be sure, but the isolation closed in on her. Indeed, this place was more prison than paradise. Would obtaining her Granny's inheritance prove too costly to spend a summer in such simplicity, solitude, and starkness?

~

William lowered the kitchen window against the rain before taking a seat across from Julia and his mother at the worn wooden dinner table. Mother passed the mashed potatoes, and he spooned a heaping mound onto his plate. Then he poured rich brown gravy liberally over it.

Julia placed a child's portion onto her plate next to a tiny piece of fish. No wonder she was so petite. She ladled a spoonful of canned beans onto her plate and stabbed a few with her fork. Her melancholy permeated the kitchen, but he held back his annoyance of it.

Her beauty, however, was another matter, one he'd ruminated over all afternoon. One that had captured his dreams ever since he'd met her at her grandmother's funeral. Despite her mood, Julia illuminated a room like the lighthouse beam itself.

Julia glanced around the unfamiliar surroundings before taking a bite, a slight furrow in her brow. She pasted on a forced smile. "This is good, Aunt Dee. Thank you." Her tone was flat. Her countenance flatter. What was so bad about being on the island?

He speared a forkful of grilled fish as Julia tentatively poked at her own plate, clearly unaccustomed to such simple fare. "I caught them just this morning. There's nothing like fresh fish."

Julia patted her lips daintily with her napkin. Her proper city manners seemed out of place in this casual island setting, and a touch of amusement mixed with a pang of empathy. The girl was definitely out of her element.

William cleared his throat and attempted to break the awkward silence that had settled between them. "What do you think of Sister Island?"

Julia's gaze flicked up, her lips quirking into a faltering smile. "It certainly is pretty." Her voice quivered. "Grandmother insisted I needed a change of scenery. A break from the hustle and bustle of the city. That's certainly true here."

He nodded, pretending to understand. What would drive a city girl like her to agree to come to a quiet place like this?

He listened as Julia and Mother conversed about Julia's grandmother, hoping to find a clue. Clearly, she loved her grandmother, and despite her obvious discomfort with being here, she spoke with determination to abide by her grandmother's wishes that she had penned in her will. Moreover, a quiet resilience seemed to infuse her. There was something undeniably intriguing about this woman.

But as she talked, her eyes and hair captivated him most. Like Mother's gingersnaps, her big round eyes held an intensity and depth that hinted at the stories and emotions within her, and her Irish roots were evident in the sprinkling of freckles that adorned her delicate skin, creating a starry map that added to her charm. A foot shorter than his own six-foot-two, with a delicate frame, she was gracefully slender.

And her tresses—a thick waterfall of ginger strands sparkling with a reddish tint, catching the early-evening light in a way that seemed almost magical. He could almost feel the softness of it under his fingertips, imagining it slipping through his hands.

"William, pass the beans, please." Mother yanked his from his musings.

He swallowed back his flusterment and handed her the bowl. "If you'll excuse me. With this rain, it's getting dark enough to light the lamp. Thank you for dinner, Mother. Julia, have a good evening."

Julia bobbed her head, licking her lips. "You, too, William. Good night." She promptly put her head down, avoiding his scrutiny.

He kissed his mother's cheek, left the room, and climbed the ladder to the lamp room. The soft rain pattered against the windowpanes as he lit the lamp, the gentle cadence adding to the quiet night in the tall tower. Up here, alone, he had time to think, to pray, to ponder. Three of his favorite pastimes.

An hour later, his mother joined him, handing him a cup of tea. "Thank you, Mother. It's just what I needed." He kissed her cheek, pleased to have her company.

For several minutes, William stood silently beside her, staring into the darkness beyond, the steam from his tea mingling with the cool air. He sipped the soothing drink, waiting for Mother to break the silence and share the concerns he sensed in her. Her countenance spoke of worry and apprehension. Whenever she looked like that, there was a story waiting to unfold.

"William, there's something I want to remind you about Julia." Mother's voice carried the burden of years gone by. "I want you to remember that she's been through more than her fair share of trials in her twenty-two years, so I urge you to have patience with her."

At the disquiet etching lines across her face, William frowned. "I know she lost her parents and grandmother."

His mother took a deep breath. "Julia lost her mother and father at the same time when she was only fourteen. A terrible accident claimed their lives, leaving her alone in this world. Can you imagine how tragic that must have been?"

He groaned with empathy and set his tea aside, giving his mother his full attention. "I forgot she was so young. I knew she lived with her granny and lost her a few months ago, but losing both her parents must have been an unimaginable tragedy for someone so young."

His mother's frown was tainted with sorrow. "Indeed, it was. Julia had to face the harsh reality of death far too soon. She became an orphan in one horrible moment, left to navigate the complexities of adolescence without the guiding hands of her parents. My friend, her granny, took her on, but the sickly woman hadn't been well for some years, so I imagine Julia had little direction growing up. And now, with her grandma gone, too, Julia has no one."

Silence lingered in the room, the reality of Julia's past settling between them like a heavy fog. Finally, Mother sighed. "It must have taken tremendous strength for Julia to overcome such a profound loss then, and now, to lose her grandmother too."

William's compassion surged. "I can't even fathom what she's going through, but I'm pleased her grandmother suggested she take a respite here for a while. I hope we can be a blessing to her."

Mother nodded, but a skeptical scowl flashed over her features. "I hope so. It may take time and patience for her to feel comfortable here. And William, her grandmother didn't just *suggest* she come here. It is a requirement for Julia to receive her inheritance."

He choked back his surprise. "Goodness. No wonder she's so melancholy."

Mother paused for a moment before continuing. "Though I don't know Julia well, I sense that she must be a remarkable young woman. But, William, please remember she carries deep scars of her past and is eight years younger than you are, so it's important that you approach her with proper judiciousness and understanding."

As the rain slowed to a sprinkle outside, William saw Julia in a new light. Though he had resolved to keep a cautious emotional distance, now he determined to be kind and supportive during her stay.

Still, that might not be so easy. After the betrayal he had experienced with his former fiancée, Louise, how could he protect himself from such an intriguing woman? Louise had left a deep, painful mark, so he had to guard his heart. He had learned the hard way that love wasn't always reciprocated—

especially when Louise jilted him for his physical challenges and soon married his best friend. After that, he had vowed to steer clear of any possible romantic entanglements, no matter what.

Yes, he would focus on offering friendship and support to Julia. But he would also carefully navigate the delicate balance between connection with her and his need for self-preservation.

He gave his mother a determined smile. "Thank you for sharing that with me. I'll do everything I can to be a friend to her."

Mother nodded, a blend of gratitude and hope in her features. "I believe you will, William. And I think Julia is blessed to have us in her life for this pivotal summer. Now, I'll take my leave. Good night, son."

Once his mother left, the soft hum of the lighthouse machinery reverberated in the tower as he stood alone, surveying the river below. The steady sweep of the beam across the water was a constant companion to his thoughts, providing comfort in the night.

As he continued to study the river below, he found himself smiling at thoughts of Julia. He was fascinated with how she moved with a certain grace, as if she glided through life with an elegance uniquely her own. And she was an artist? Oh, how he longed to see her at work, to watch her create a masterpiece on his island.

There was much to learn about her—of that, he was sure.

Lost in his contemplation, William's heart swelled with curiosity. In that quiet moment, with the river stretching out before him, he silently vowed that, while keeping her at a safe distance, he would be a steady light in her life, just as the lighthouse was for the ships navigating the waters below.

The hatch to the lighthouse tower creaked open, and Julia's head appeared against the soft shine of the lantern room, a genial smile greeting him as he put out his hand and helped her climb the ladder and step inside.

The light emanating from the huge lamp caught her attention. "Goodness! I didn't realize how bright it is up here. It's dazzling."

"The fixed white light has a sixth-order Fresnel lens, so it projects a brilliant beam."

"And warmth." She swiped her brow with her shirtsleeve, and her voice, soft in the quiet space, sounded almost like a little girl's. "I thought I'd check in before retiring for the night. Do you need anything?"

He appreciated her thoughtfulness but shook his head and motioned to his mug. "No, I'm fine, thank you. Mother already brought me tea."

Julia looked out the windows into the dark night. "It's beautiful up here. I can see why you enjoy your work."

He gestured for her to take a seat on the narrow bench. "You're welcome to join me for a few minutes."

Julia smiled and took a seat on the bench, the scent of her tangy lemon verbena tickling his nose. As he settled next to her, their shoulders almost touching, they looked out at the expansive night sky. The rain clouds had scattered, so the stars above poked through and twinkled like distant diamonds, and the moon radiated a silvery glimmer on the river below.

"I've always loved the night sky, but out here, it's so much darker and the stars more visible than in the city." Julia's face reflected the awe of the celestial display. "I would love to paint it one evening."

"Indeed. To me, the heavens are like a home for unspoken dreams. And the view from up here in the lighthouse is a little piece of heaven."

The measured pulse of the beam created a soothing cadence, and faint scent of the river filled the air. Julia's close proximity set his pulse to quicken and beads of sweat to his brow.

"Do you like being a lightkeeper?"

William motioned toward the steady illumination emanating from the lens. "I find comfort in the light. It reminds me that even in the darkest of nights, there's something constant and reassuring."

Julia groaned, a long whoosh of breath following. "I wish there was something steady and inspiring for me, like this beacon is to you. But I find no comfort in the vastness of the days of uncertainty ahead of me. Instead, the emptiness of being alone shakes me to my core."

William touched her hand, patting it cautiously. "You're never alone, Julia. God said, 'I am always with you, even to the end of the world.'"

Julia blinked at his touch and shook her head. She tugged her hands into a tight ball close to her body. "I don't know that God or that peaceful feeling."

William had no response to that. It was the first time he'd ever met someone without faith like his. But Julia needed someone's help to navigate the dark and lonely waters within her. He sensed her bitterness, her hopelessness, her need of healing. But without God, how could he come to her aid?

If you love historical romance, check out the other Wild Heart books!

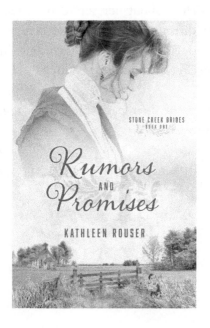

Rumors and Promises by Kathleen Rouser

She's an heiress hiding a tumultuous past. He's a reverend desperate to atone for his failures.

Abandoned by her family, Sophie Biddle has been on the run with a child in tow. At last, she's found a safe life in Stone Creek, Michigan, teaching piano. But when a kind, yet meddling and handsome, minister walks into her life seeking to help, Sophie is caught off guard and wary. When her secrets threaten to be exposed, will she be able to trust the reverend, and more importantly, God?

After failing his former flock, Reverend Ian McCormick is determined to start anew in Stone Creek, and he's been working harder than ever to forget his mistakes and prove himself to his new congregation—and to God. But when he meets a young woman seeking acceptance and respect, despite the rumors swirling about her sordid past, Ian finds himself pulled in two directions. If he shows concern for Sophie's plight, he could risk everything—including his position as pastor of Stone Creek Community Church.

Will the scandals of their pasts bind them together or drive them apart forever?

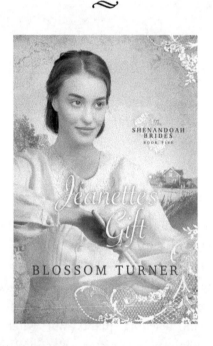

Jeanette's Gift by Blossom Turner

This life wasn't the one she dreamed of, but happily ever afters don't always come when and how we expect.

At twenty-nine, Jeanette Williams has watched each one of her four sisters marry and start families of their own. It's hard not to believe God has forgotten the desires of her heart, especially when most people refer to her as Spinster Williams. Without the beautiful children she teaches, life would be unbearably lonely.

When the handsome widower, Theo Wallace, and his six children move into the Shenandoah Valley, every available woman is atwitter—except for Jeanette. She has no such aspirations that someone as plain as her could draw even a smattering of interest.

As life throws this unlikely couple together, Jeanette can't help but fall in love with Theo's children and their soul-wrenching plight. Before she knows it, her heart is far more invested than she could've ever imagined. And not just with the children, but with their handsome father as well. Is she headed for another heartbreak, or is it possible God had a beautiful plan in the works all along?

∾

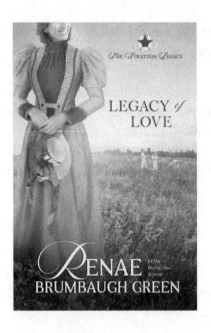

Legacy of Love by Renae Brumbaugh Green

She's struggled her entire life to overcome her parentage.

Skye Stratton is nearly perfect. Or at least, she tries to be. She carries the Stratton name, but everyone knows her true half-breed heritage. When she completes her education and is hired as a teacher at the local school, she hopes to finally find acceptance in the town. But when most of her class elects to stay home rather than be taught by an Indian, she knows things will never change.

Alan McNaughten went to Washington, D.C. to make a difference. Instead, he finds himself entrenched in political lies, manipulation, and deceit. When he finds a way to return home to Texas as an Indian Agent, he leaps at the chance. Even if he must hurt an innocent woman to secure his position.

But when the lovely Miss Stratton agrees to teach for the Alabama-Coushatta Reservation, Alan knows he's gone too far. He'll do anything to protect her from further heartache and harm. But what will happen when she learns the truth about her position...and the truth about him?